TALES FROM THE ISLE OF IONA

— *Episode One* —
Coracle and the Lost Cave

by
Odell A. Scott

PublishAmerica
Baltimore

© 2004 by Odell A. Scott.
All rights reserved. No part of this book may be reproduced, stored in a retrieval system, or transmitted in any form or by any means without the prior written permission of the publishers, except by a reviewer who may quote brief passages in a review to be printed in a newspaper, magazine, or journal.

First printing

ISBN: 1-4137-3045-0
PUBLISHED BY PUBLISHAMERICA, LLLP
www.publishamerica.com
Baltimore

Printed in the United States of America

To Bobbi, Andrew and Amelia

— Contents —

Part One

Chapter 1 • My Own World • 9
Chapter 2 • Markers and Directions • 19
Chapter 3 • Somebody's Joke • 24
Chapter 4 • Back Here Again • 28

Part Two

Chapter 5 • In Just 12 Short Days • 37
Chapter 6 • The Last Marker • 49
Chapter 7 • The Famous Inventor • 63
Chapter 8 • Our New Best Friend • 69
Chapter 9 • The Plan • 86
Chapter 10 • Andrew Becomes a Believer • 91
Chapter 11 • In over Our Heads • 105
Chapter 12 • The Plan Revisited • 110
Chapter 13 • It Looked Easy on Paper • 118
Chapter 14 • Home Away from Home • 126
Chapter 15 • Dreams Are Funny That Way • 134
Chapter 16 • Grave Digging? You're Joking! • 144
Chapter 17 • Those Scary Eyes • 153
Chapter 18 • Will He Stay or Will He Go? • 161
Chapter 19 • Laying Down the Law and Letting Go • 173
Chapter 20 • Forgiveness and Good Beer • 179
Chapter 21 • A Trip They'll Never Forget • 187
Chapter 22 • He's on His Way … and We're on Ours • 193
Chapter 23 • A Singing Sensation • 199
Chapter 24 • My New Family • 204

Come with me and uncover the ancient mysteries hidden in the fog of Scotland's past.

— PART ONE —

— 1 —

MY OWN WORLD

"Neil, Neil! Wake up!" My mother was shaking me out of a sound sleep.

"What is it?" I slowly opened my eyes.

"They're on their way! You need to get up and put your clothes on. Light your beacons and don't forget your torch. They said you have only five minutes before the planes get here."

I pulled on my pants and shirt, grabbed my coat, picked up my torch, and was out the door in minutes. As I raced down the street, I could feel the cold, damp air replacing the warmth from my bed, but I didn't care. People's lives were depending on me.

I was out of breath, my mouth was dry, and my muscles were aching. I could feel a trickle of sweat running down my back as I made my way to the top of the hill where my signal barrels waited. I tore off the lids, ignited the torch, and touched it to the liquid in the barrel. *Swoosh!* The flames jumped about four feet in the air. Startled, I fell backward and rapidly crawled crab-like away from the flames. They must have changed the mixture in the barrels; the flames were never that high before.

"It's about time you got here, Neil!" old man McDuff yelled from the next hill over. He always had his barrels lit before mine. I wondered if he ever left his post.

I sat down in the long grass; I could hear the droning of the engines in the distance. They were getting louder as each second passed. I stood and looked south. It was quite a sight to see the many signal fires outlining the entire east coast of our little island.

If only I were a few years older, I could be a pilot. I imagined myself flying through heavy flak, evading enemy fighters and looking for cloud cover. Then, at the right moment, I'd dive to the target, dropping my bombs and bringing the plane back safe and sound. There wasn't much to do while manning the signal fires and waiting for the planes to pass, except try to keep warm and make up stories. I pretended I knew what mission our boys were completing.

I was sure that the airplanes I now saw in the distance were on their way back from a bombing run in Germany, probably a top-secret mission. I wondered what kind of resistance they had run into.

You could always tell our planes by the sound of them passing overhead. My mother said the engines frightened her, but I thought they purred like a contented cat. They were getting closer, and I could see that the interior lights were on.

They flew lower now, just two or three hundred feet above us. Not only were they extremely loud, but you could smell the exhaust and feel the wind blow over your head as they passed. I always carried a flag of Scotland in my pocket, and I would wave it at the planes as they flew by. Some of the older boys said the pilots would drop candy bars if they saw you and were close enough, but I haven't been that lucky. Or maybe they were just pulling my leg. You know how older kids are.

I pulled my journal from my back pocket. I used it to keep track of the number of planes and their formations each time I was out here. I counted twenty bombers as they passed and faded into the distance. I made a note on the bottom of the page that these planes were on their way back to a secret airstrip somewhere in Scotland. I also noted that it must have been a successful mission: no stalled or sputtering engines, no smoke or fire.

After the planes were out of sight, I put the tops back on my barrels and stood for a moment looking down the coastline. The signal fires went out one by one until there was no way to tell the sea from land. I listened to the waves breaking in the distance and felt the sea air rush by my face. I never looked forward to putting out the fires in the barrels. That meant the excitement was over, and I was left with my thoughts and fears about the war. I wondered how my dad was doing and if he would make it home. Those concerns were hard to deal with sometimes, and I was glad there was someway I could do my part for the war.

The year is 1944. World War II is raging in Europe and Asia. Our fathers and older brothers are away from home fighting the Germans. My mom, dad, and I live on Iona. Our beautiful island off the coast of Scotland is roughly one mile wide and three and a half miles long. Yes, it's very small, but there are many golden beaches and hidden coves for exploring. A carpet of emerald green grass covers the island most of the year. In school we learned that this island has some of the oldest rocks in the world, some dating back three thousand million years.

Iona and Mull were part of Greenland until they split and drifted apart a long time ago, creating separate islands. There is evidence that Iona has been continually inhabited since the last ice age ended. Hunters and gatherers lived in the caves here and on Mull. I wondered why anyone would want to live here when there is so much more close by.

We are famous for the Abbey, the Nunnery, and Reilig Odhrain– the old cemetery where over forty Scottish kings are said to be buried. A priest named Columbia founded the Abbey in A.D. 575. I've been told that when he was traveling from Ireland to Scotland to bring Christianity to the clans, he was forced to take refuge from a storm. (At that time, it was common to travel hundreds of miles in a cigar-shaped boat called a coracle. Our class in school thought the boat looked like a combination of a kayak and a small submarine. Our teacher said that no one was quite sure where the design for that type of boat came from.) He was so moved from the moment he landed on the beach that he decided it would be a special place to meditate and think. So he built a church. Others must have agreed, for more buildings quickly followed. To this day, many artifacts and ancient buildings can be found around the Abbey.

Yes, people have long regarded this little island as a special place. People from all over the world visit the Abbey and Nunnery during the summer. Because there are only a few places for them to stay overnight, the ferry usually drops them off in the morning and picks them up in the late afternoon.

I can't understand why so few people venture to the more remote parts of the island. (My dad says I should be happy they don't.) I think the beaches and coves are as interesting as any old building. Perhaps nobody goes far from the main coastal attractions because there are only a couple of roads, and they only cover the eastern side of the island. If you want to see the western side, you have to walk on a number of small paths. You also have to bring your own food and drinks because there aren't any stores or restaurants.

Normally the island population is about four hundred, but with the war, there are less than two hundred people living here now. My mum says our island is safe because there is nothing here worth bombing, and it's protected by ancient spirits. I just nod my head. Nothing worth bombing and nothing worth doing is more like it. In the library I read the newspapers from London and Glasgow, and it sure seems I'm missing out on what's going on.

Speaking of isolation, we live in a small two-story fieldstone house about half a mile from the town center. Some might think our house and yard would make a great postcard. A stone fence, made from local rock, borders the front and sides of our property, and the front yard has a few old trees. When you enter the front door, you step down a few feet. The house is built down into the earth, supposedly to help with the heating and cooling. I just know that it makes the house look small from the outside, and visitors are always surprised by how big the rooms feel.

I like my upstairs bedroom, which has enough room for all my things. One day I was complaining that there was no place to display my many collections, so my dad and I built some shelves and a secret compartment in the wall.

Hidden behind a picture of an old sailing ship, that's where I keep my most valuable possessions.

Dad lets me help him with chores and repairs around the house. I have always enjoyed working with tools and will take every opportunity to build or fix things, sometimes whether they need it or not. I seem to have a sixth sense when it comes to mechanical things. It's as though I can see the sequence of steps needed to take things apart. Dad says he thinks I should become an engineer. I think being a pilot sounds more exciting.

Sometimes before bed time Dad would tell me facts and stories about Iona. He told me that this is a special place to live and that history could be exciting. He said our house is over three hundred years old and showed me some old drawings and documents. Unfortunately, it was lost on me at the time.

There have been many improvements to the house over the years. With the exception of close neighbors, we have all the modern conveniences. The nearest homes are in the town center, where all my friends live. Their parents work in the many shops, the Abbey, or for the government. My dad works for the local ferry, the Caledonian MacBrayne, which travels back and forth between Mull and Iona. He learned all about boats when he was in the Navy for five years. Afterward, he and some friends decided to work for the ferry company. He said that although it wasn't exactly sailing, at least it kept him close to the sea.

I remember asking him why we live out in the country.

He said that he and my mum had looked at houses in town when his company transferred him to Iona. They were about to settle on one when the realtor told them about this house. She was sure they wouldn't be interested, but she was wrong. Dad told me that both he and Mum fell in love with the place as soon as they saw it. I guess when you're older you think differently.

Ever since my dad had to go back in the Navy because of war, life has been very different. I never realized or even thought about how he fit into our family. My mum is great, but when my dad's around, the house has a whole different feel. He also did many chores I wasn't aware of. But I am now.

Now that it's just my mum and me, we have gotten to know each other on a completely new level, more like equals. I've asked her lots of questions about how she met dad, what they did before I was born, stuff like that. One day she told me that I was a miracle baby. The doctor had told her that the chances of her ever having children were remote. And just when they were resigned to that fact, I came along. She and dad wanted to have more children, but it wasn't meant to be. When I asked her why I had green eyes when she and Dad didn't, she just shrugged her shoulders and said, "Who knows?" When I asked questions about why she couldn't have more children, she would change the subject. I finally got the message: girl stuff. Most of the time we acted more like friends than mother and son, but whenever I started to push it, she let me know that she was still in charge.

With all the turmoil and changes that have occurred because of the war, school has become the main focus of my life. It's where my friends and I escape into our own little world of make-believe. Most of us are in the same situation with brothers or a dad serving in the armed forces. On this island, you become good friends with your schoolmates. Something about living on an island draws people together, and war makes that tendency even more intense.

Every Monday morning, school begins with our teacher calling us to order. She then reads us an article about one of the latest battles, or sometimes just general war information. Regardless, the message is clear about how we are beating back the enemy, and that victory is around the corner.

We all get letters from our fathers and brothers, letting us know what is going on with them. The way they tell it doesn't always sound like what we hear at school. We suspect that the school reports leave out some of the facts. But what really bothers me about the war is that we're on this little island with no bridges, and the ferry service is down to once a week, so there is nowhere to go and even less to do.

Slap! The teacher's ruler hits the desk. "Are you boys listening?" She glares at us with her piercing green eyes. Of course we weren't paying attention. It was almost time to leave for the day. Our fourth grade teacher Miss Abernathy is always in a bad mood. "Don't forget to finish reading chapter ten in your English book," she says curtly. "We'll discuss it tomorrow."

The three o'clock bell rang, and we rushed to jam our books in our backpacks. We were in the hallway putting our jackets on when I shouted to a couple of my mates dawdling by the water fountain. "Come on, you don't want to be late!"

Today, like every other Wednesday, we were walking over to visit Eagon's great-grandfather, who looks about a hundred years old. Even though we think we're almost grown up, we still look forward to him telling us stories about what our island was like in ancient times. Some of his stories are scary, almost as scary as he is. We feel all right with him as long as we're in a group, but if you were alone with him, you would always be wondering …

His strange living quarters were a kid's dream. His apartment is connected by a tunnel located in the back of Eagon's house. Once in the house, you'd walk through a small door off the main kitchen, which always smelled of fresh bread, then down a dark hallway tunnel that always smelled like wet dirt. We'd run our hands along the almost smooth rock walls as we headed through the dimly lit passageway. At the end of the tunnel was a huge wooden door that opened up to a great room. The room has to be carved into the side of the hill, because you can't see any outer walls when you're outside.

As you walk through the doorway and enter the living room area, the first thing you notice is the domed ceiling with crisscrossed wooden beams. In the center of the squares are paintings of battle scenes and landscapes of the island. They have turned yellowish-brown with age, some are cracked, and many have pieces missing.

On the back wall is a hearth made of large stones that have been cut to fit together perfectly, and the firebox is big enough for me to walk into. The light from the fire flickers on the entire room, giving it an eerie feel. There are lamps throughout the room, but they are never on when we're there. I think Eagon's granddad keeps them off to set the mood. Believe me, it works.

He is usually smoking his pipe as he waits for us in his rocking chair. I think the rocking chair was created out of one giant piece of wood. It has wide arms with serpent heads carved at the ends. I don't like to look at them because sometimes the flickering light from the fireplace makes the faces seem alive. Although the old man doesn't answer many questions about his past, Eagon says he was a fisherman until his boat was destroyed in a big storm a long time ago.

We'd all grab pillows and take our positions around his chair, the fire roaring and crackling behind us, bits of yellow light jumping all over the room. Even after we were settled, he'd continue smoking and pretending he didn't see us. We'd all start begging, "Start the story … please." He would then look up at the ceiling, scratch his beard, and look each of us in the eyes.

The stories always started out the same way. Long ago, a tribe of people lived right here in a village next to St. Ronan's Bay. No one knows where they came from or where they went. In today's story, the villagers were preparing for the winter season. Some people were bundling reeds and grasses and some were packing dried fish into baskets when a lookout ran into the village shouting, "They are coming! Looks like more than twenty long boats!"

They were about to be attacked by a Viking raiding party much larger than their village population. The only chance they had was to hide. Everyone gathered in front of the chief's hut to tell him about the size of the force and ask for his help. He told them to gather their belongings, and then he guided them to a nearby hillside where he prayed to the gods near a special rock. On his command, part of the rock slid to one side. The chief guided the stunned village people inside and closed the entrance. They stayed inside until the Vikings had left their village.

The story went on with details about other battles and skirmishes with the Vikings. He told us that the local people had many secret ceremonies and sacred holidays that brought them together and kept them safe.

As we listened, we helped ourselves to fresh bread and cheese from the top of an old wooden table next to the fireplace. Before we knew it, it was six o'clock and time for us to go home.

There were a few other adults in town that we sometimes visited, but our favorite and most profitable day was always at the Inventor's workshop. At the end of each week, we did odd jobs for him. His name was George Beaton, but everybody on the island called him the Inventor. Nobody seemed to know much about him. He was always polite but kept to himself. The attitude of most adults on this island was that as long as he didn't cause trouble he could act however he wanted. That doesn't mean people weren't curious, but being judgmental could get you in trouble on Iona. Just about everybody who lived on this island was a character and had some personal secrets.

Friday after school and sometimes on Saturday, we would go to his house and help him clean up his workshop.

He lived at the end of an isolated road; his nearest neighbor was half a mile away. He was always in the process of building something. There were materials and tools everywhere. We actually enjoyed cleaning up his mess.

It's funny how I got this job. One day at school the principal called me into his office. That would have scared me normally, but I'd had a dream the night before. I could almost remember it. Something good happened to me, but all the details were just out of reach. It has been my experience that when I have those kind of dreams, something good happens to me the next day. Knowing this, I proceeded to the principal's office without fear and took a seat in front of his desk.

"I have a note for you," the principal said. "George Beaton dropped it off this morning. He needs a few kids to help him clean up around his workshop, and he thought of you first." He handed me the note. "Here are the details."

I read the letter, which listed the work he wanted done. He said I could bring a few of my trusted friends. He also mentioned the days he wanted help and how much he would pay us. I was very excited and chose a few of my best mates to join me. I was curious how he knew about me because I had never met him. I told my mum about it when I got home that day, she just smiled and said that it's a small island. As I expected, she told me to behave myself and do a good job.

After we finished cleaning up the first time, I asked the Inventor why he picked me. He said that he saw me around, and I looked like a trustworthy boy. It was as good as answer as any, I guess. His letter is one of the things I keep in my secret compartment behind the picture in my room.

— 2 —

MARKERS AND DIRECTIONS

    The afternoon school bell rang at three o'clock on Friday, finally the last day of school for the year. We didn't have to think about Miss Abernathy, read boring books, or do homework until next term. We were free! We grabbed our notebooks, supplies, and school projects before running out the door. It was summer break, and we were on our way to the Inventor's house.
    As we walked down the road, Malcolm asked what we thought the Inventor would be working on today. We just shrugged. Although we asked, the Inventor never talked much about his projects. We got the impression that the subject was off limits because he always avoided answering when we asked him anything. All we ever saw were the leftover parts and the mess; I figured he did the final assembly in another building. We didn't really care. We were just happy to have a job cleaning up his workshop, which consisted mostly of sweeping and throwing out garbage. At least we were earning money, which was very hard to come by at that time.

* * *

We stood on his front porch, each of us taking a turn knocking on the door. "He doesn't seem to be home," I said. "Lets go see if he's around back in the workshop."

"Sounds like a good idea," Fergus whispered. "We don't want to miss a payday."

There are two buildings in the back of the house. We had to walk past the smaller of the two before we reached the one we were to clean. None of us had ever been in the smaller one. As we were headed toward the workshop, Fergus noticed that the door to the smaller building was open. He was in the rear of our group, so no one was aware when he made a detour to peek inside. Suddenly he was shouting, "Hey, mates! You have to see what's in there!" We turned, saw the open door and rushed to see what he was talking about.

From the outside, the building looked rundown, but the inside had been converted into a first-class workshop. On one wall were hundreds of tools neatly arranged by size and type. In the center of the floor were white canvases covering three ghostly shaped objects, one large and two small. The other side of the shop was vintage Inventor material a mess of boxes, pictures, and spare parts. We entered, staring in amazement at the half-finished contraptions. So this is where he assembled all the parts he built in the other workshop.

Fergus pulled the canvas off the largest covered object. "Do you think this really flies?" he asked as we stepped in for a closer look.

"It looks like a personal helicopter," I said.

Fergus jumped into the seat and started playing with the controls. He made gun noises with his mouth, pretending to shoot down enemy planes. I knew nothing good could come from this. He was really getting into his fantasy, making a motor sound with his mouth. In his excitement he flicked a switch on the control panel in front of him. A moment later there was a loud clicking sound, and the rotors started to move.

"Turn it off before you break something!" I yelled. It was too late. The rotors started turning. We didn't know that one of the blades had not been bolted into place. The rotor gained speed quickly, and the loose blade sailed across the room, becoming lodged in the wall opposite the machine. Fergus finally turned off the switch, and the blades came to a stop. Everybody froze.

I knew I had to do something so I picked up a chair and ran over to the wall. Standing on the chair, I pulled and the blade came out of the wall. "Come on, a little help here," I said in a shaky voice. "Let's put it back where it belongs. If we do this right, he'll never know." I handed the blade to Fergus, and he and the others pushed the blade back into the rotor housing. They threw the canvas back over the top of the machine so it looked like no one had disturbed it. "That looks good," I said.

We then turned our attention to the hole in the wall. I climbed back up on the chair to examine the area. "It's not that big," I said. "I think we can patch it so he won't notice."

"How?" asked Fergus. "It's pretty good sized. Even if we can find some plaster, we'd never be able to match the color with the rest of the wall."

I looked around and saw a stack of pictures leaning against the wall. "How about if we hang a picture over the hole? I doubt he ever looks at anything in here besides his machines."

"That's the first good idea you've had in a long time," said Eagon.

Fergus found a picture large enough to cover the hole and handed it to me. I glanced into the hole as I was looking for the best place to drive the nail. "Hey, there is something behind this wall."

"Like what?" asked Eagon.

"It looks like a bookshelf."

"Anything on it?"

"Yeah, a book."

"Grab it and bring it down here," Eagon said.

I stretched my arm into the opening and brought out the book. I handed it down to him, and he took it to an empty table. We all gathered around as he opened it. The book was ancient. The pages looked and felt like old leather. "What language is this?" Fergus wondered aloud.

"I don't know," I replied. "I've never seen anything like it. They aren't letters. They're more like symbols, like Chinese writing."

There was a small bookmark near the center of the book, and Eagon carefully opened it up. "It looks like a map of this area. Look! There's the harbor … and Calf Island." He pointed to the page excitedly. "This look like a marker, and this arrow-like thing must be showing a direction."

"Maybe it's a treasure map," I said.

"What else would it be?" Furgus replied.

"Let's get some paper and copy the map," I said. "Then we can put the book back, hang the picture, and hope for the best." Everyone agreed.

Furgus pulled a notebook from his backpack and carefully copied the map, making sure he had all the details. When he was finished, we quickly returned the book to its place behind the wall and hung the picture over the hole. I was the last to leave. Before I closed the door to the workshop, I looked around to make sure there was no trace that we had been there. It looked exactly as we had found it, except for the picture.

We waited outside the door of the other building for another fifteen minutes, but the inventor did not appear.

We finally wrote him a note to let him know we'd be back the following day about nine o'clock to help him straighten up. I stuck it to the door with a piece of my bubble gum.

As we started back down the road, Eagon said, "Is anyone else afraid to come back here tomorrow? What if he sees what we did? What if he yells and we lose our jobs?"

"We did a good job of covering up. We have to act natural, like nothing happened, or he will get suspicious." I tried to sound confident. We all agreed there was no way we'd get caught. The conversation quickly turned to the book and the map.

"Maybe," Eagon said, "the people who wrote it were ancient pirates from China. Maybe the past owner of this house found the book and hid it. Maybe he forgot about it … or maybe he died. Even if that isn't true, and the Inventor knows about it, the book is still there so we aren't in trouble."

"Just think what could be buried right here on this island!" Fergus broke in.

We all went home daydreaming of the treasure map and what we'd buy with the gold and jewels we would find. Those happy thoughts, however, were periodically invaded by fear about what would happen if the Inventor noticed the hole in the wall.

Right before I fell asleep, I decided that if this was any indication of things to come, it was going to be a memorable summer vacation.

* * *

The next morning we met at the Inventor's house, he gave us instructions and cleaned as usual. To our great relief, he never said a thing about the hole in the wall.

After we finished our chores and received our pay, we were on our way to the little store in the village to buy candy with our wages. As soon as the Inventor's house was out of sight, we started to talk about how we should search for the treasure. Each of us put forth a plan of action, but we couldn't determine which was best. We finally agreed to meet the next day after church to begin searching for the first marker.

— 3 —

SOMEBODY'S JOKE

Sunday afternoon we all gathered under the enormous old tree at the end of the road. Fergus took charge, belting out orders like a drill sergeant. "The first marker looks like it's near a large grove of trees on the northern part of the island! We need to find a large stone with strange markings on it, and an arrow pointing the direction of the next marker. Let's go!" Everyone broke into a trot.

When we reached the area where the grove of trees should be, there were no trees. As our group slowly assembled, Fergus opened the map again.

"I'm sure those trees were cut down hundreds of years ago," said Malcolm, looking around.

We broke up, each of us taking a different direction as we looked for the stone marker. Dirt began flying as we cleared away grasses and brush from areas where we thought the marker was likely to be buried.

Near the end of the day, Eagon saw a partially covered rock, and he called us to help him uncover it. We were all tired of looking on our own so Eagon's request was a welcome change of pace. It took awhile to pull away the dirt and small pebbles, but when some of the rock was exposed, it looked like something had been carved into it.

We dug even faster.

After about forty-five minutes of hard work, we stood, breathing hard and staring at the uncovered rock.

"It's unbelievable," I panted. "We found the first marker. It has symbols just like the one on the map. And that arrow is pointing west."

It was nearing five o'clock, and we needed to head home for supper. As we walked back, we talked about how easy it was to find the first marker. At this rate, we all thought we could surely find the treasure by the end of the week.

In the middle of our speculations about what kind of treasure we would find, Furgus blurted out, "You know what always happens in the movies when people find treasure?"

"What?" said Eagon.

"Everyone gets greedy and starts fighting with each other to get all the treasure for themselves."

"That's not going to happen to us," I said. We stopped walking and I put my hand out. "Come on, let's swear." We formed a circle and each of us put our hands on top of the others as we all swore to share equally in anything we might find. We felt more like a team as we continued our walk home.

Then I had an idea. "How about if we pool part of our shares and buy ourselves a boat that we can all use?" Everyone agreed that that was the first thing we would buy. Then we could leave the island whenever we wanted to. We were sure, too, that there would be plenty of money for other things we wanted.

We were all in good spirits when we reached the point where we went our separate ways. It had been a great day. We decided to meet at the stone marker first thing in the morning to continue the quest for the second marker.

* * *

The next morning we gathered at the first marker and moved in the direction the arrow pointed. We were to be looking for the base of a stone tower, which was near the location of the second marker. We didn't have any luck that day.

We would try again over the next few days, searching repeatedly in what looked like the right area, but it was a dead end. We could not find any of the landmarks pictured on the map.

It was summer, and a bunch of ten and eleven year olds didn't have the patience for walking around in circles and not finding anything. One by one, we began losing interest in searching for the markers and the dream of treasure, along with our plans for a boat.

On Friday we cleaned the Inventor's workshop and then walked to the little store to buy some ice cream. Our conversation was going back and forth between the war and the Inventor when out of nowhere Eagon said, "Maybe there was only one marker and the treasure map was somebody's joke, or maybe it wasn't really a treasure map at all. I'm tired of looking for the second marker. Besides, the annual summer fair is in a few weeks." He pointed to a poster tacked on the side of a building. We all felt the same way about the map, but no one had wanted to be the first to give up. Thank God Eagon had said it. And we'd all have large roles in the summer fair because so many adults were away serving in the war. It would be best to wait until at least after the fair to look for treasure.

For the rest of that summer, we made do with visiting the usual people and places on Iona. As the war raged on to our east, we lit signal fires and helped out wherever we could. We listened to Eagon's great grandfather's stories and cleaned up the Inventor's workshop. We bought lots of ice cream, and some of us dreamed of what it would be like to live somewhere other than this island.

*　*　*

When I awoke one Saturday late in October, I felt a heavy sense of dread from the moment I opened my eyes. It was like I had eaten something bad. The feeling wouldn't leave me. Late that afternoon the war became very real for my mom and me.

Military officers knocked on our door. I saw their jeep from my upstairs bedroom window. When I heard mom start crying, I knew my dad wasn't ever coming back.

— 4 —

BACK HERE AGAIN

Many years have passed, and here I am sitting in the kitchen of what used to be the Inventor's house, sipping a cup of tea and thinking how strange life is.

After high school I left Iona and made a life for myself on Mull. But after many years, here I am living on Iona again. There's no way I could have predicted the unbelievable string of events that have occurred since my son Colin and I left Mull only two months ago.

I remember how I felt as a kid living here, and how much I wanted to leave and travel the world. When I was Colin's age, I thought there was very little excitement in my life. Sometimes time seemed to stand still. I can say with certainty that Colin will never have those feelings about his youth here on Iona.

I guess I've gotten ahead of myself. Let me back up a bit…

* * *

I remember the excitement in the air after my high school graduation. By late summer, nearly everyone in our class had left to follow their dreams. A few of my friends got jobs in town; they loved Iona and wanted to stay. The rest of us couldn't wait to leave. We moved to nearby islands or the mainland of Scotland.

I moved to the city of Craignure on the Isle of Mull mainly because it wasn't Iona. It had more people and was more exciting. Also, I had enrolled in a very good trade school there; I thought I wanted to be an auto mechanic. I completed the course and got a job in a Ford garage. That lasted about six months. I liked fixing cars and was good at it, but it wasn't enough. It just didn't feel right.

I tried many different occupations after that: carpenter, bricklayer, plumber. I didn't last at any of them because I wasn't driven and simply lost interest after a while. The common thread in all those jobs was that I liked the challenge of a puzzle, finding the problem and then fixing it.

While looking for my next career, I took a job at the largest hardware store in town, on a temporary basis, of course. Interestingly, I ended up liking it and the people I worked with. Things just seemed to work out, and I quickly worked my way up to store manager.

During my time at the store, I met a local girl named Ann. We fell in love and married. We got along well and enjoyed being with each other. I took Ann to see my mom after we were married. Mom was very sick, but happy that I had met someone and was settling down. It was at that time that I reluctantly sold the house I grew up in and moved Mom to a group care home. Some months later her sickness continued to worsen, and she was transferred to the local hospital. If she could have lived a few more months, she would have seen our baby boy.

Unfortunately, that was not the end of the personal tragedies I would experience. I started to think I was cursed when my wife died of childbirth complications. I was left to raise our son Colin by myself.

It's difficult to remember anything in particular during the next few years. I had so many painful emotions rolling around in my head that I eventually blocked most everything out.

As I mentioned, I was an only child, but luckily for me, my wife had two brothers and a sister. All of them had large families that lived close by, and they welcomed Colin and me into their homes. Having lots of people around was a lifesaver for us.

Quite in contrast to my earlier years of restlessness, I had grown to enjoy my life, which consisted mostly of work and family events. My younger fantasies of taking off and traveling to every country of the world were confined to my dreams.

Then everything changed. I will never forget that night about three months ago. I had some very vivid dreams that woke me, and I knew that something big was going to happen. That sixth sense I'd had as a child hadn't waned. It had always given me advance warning that something in my life was about to change. It told me when I was going to be leaving a job or if a new opportunity was coming my way, and so forth.

It had been an uneventful Tuesday. After I picked Colin up from a friend's house, we had dinner, played a game, and then went to bed. I awoke from a restless sleep at 2:00 A.M. with an uneasy feeling that wouldn't let me fall back asleep. I knew I'd had a troubling dream, but I couldn't remember what it was about. Things had been fine, so I had no idea what could be keeping me up. I think I fell back asleep at about 4:00 A.M. I slept right through the alarm, and Colin was shaking me a few hours later.

That was a big day for me. It was my tenth anniversary at the hardware store, and as was the custom, my co-workers were taking me out to lunch to celebrate.

I arrived at work on time and attended to the customers. When there was a lull in the action, I took my place at the front counter and began sorting through the day's orders while having my third cup of coffee.

I saw the postman coming through the front door to drop off envelopes and small packages. It was my daily ritual before lunch to sort through the usual bills and junk mail for the store. That day I'd been hoping for a specific parts catalog.

He handed me the stack and I walked to my office. As I began flipping through the large armful of mail, one letter jumped out of the stack. The envelope was addressed to me personally. The paper stock was fancy, my name was written by a polished hand, and I noticed that the postmark was from Iona. I looked at the return address: William Jeffries, Solicitor. Did I go to school with him?

I put down the other letters and was about to open it when my workmates gathered around the door, pointing to their watches. "It's lunchtime," one of them said. "Let's go. We only have an hour." I put the letter in the top drawer of my desk, thinking I'd read it later.

I grabbed my coat and turned my attention to lunch. An hour and a half later we returned feeling full, happy, and a little tipsy from the Belhaven Ale. I was never much of a drinker.

On my way back into the store, I passed the order inbox; the large stack of new orders waiting to be processed was impossible for me to ignore. I grabbed the pile and started to sort through them, looking for any last minute afternoon deliveries that had to be made. I was halfway through them when I saw an order from a law firm, which reminded me of the letter I had placed in my drawer before lunch. Putting the orders aside, I walked into my office and retrieved the letter. I stared at it again before quickly opening it.

It was from the Inventor's solicitor. Strange. I hadn't thought about George Beaton in years. I continued reading. Apparently, the Inventor had died suddenly. In his will, he left his house, workshops, and property to me, Neil Pinnington. There was one stipulation: to execute the will, I must be living in the house two weeks upon receipt of the letter. The solicitor would meet me at the house on August fourth to finalize all the legal paperwork.

I dropped the letter on the desk and stared straight ahead. Why would the Inventor give me his house? Two weeks? I have two weeks to decide ... and move? I turned the papers over and examined them. They sure looked real enough.

I started thinking about the pros and cons of returning to Iona. I'm definitely not having the kind of life I had imagined when I made plans many years ago. I'd been at this job for a decade, doing pretty much the same thing week after week. I didn't see that changing much in the near future. I did have Colin to consider; it would be a big adjustment for him. But I'd grown up on the island and had a good life (I could see that in retrospect), and he would only be a ferry ride away from visiting his cousins. A house with property would be better than the attached flat we have right now. I wondered what inventions George had tucked away in those back buildings. Could I really live there? What would I do for a living?

The thoughts were racing through my mind, one after another. I knew this would be a big decision, and it would change our lives. I also knew that I hadn't been this excited about something in years.

Two hours had passed since I had opened the letter and read the news. I was trying to be an adult about evaluating this opportunity. I knew I shouldn't make the decision too fast, but I felt it would be crazy not to jump at it. I told myself that I could always sell the place and come back to Mull if I wanted. That decided it.

I couldn't wait until I was home to call and confirm that the offer was real, so I phoned the solicitor from my office. He confirmed it. As long as I met the stipulation of living in the house in two weeks, it was mine. I felt like I had won the lottery. I could hardly contain myself as I completed the rest of my shift at the store.

At dinner that night I told Colin what had happened. I started telling him about the adventures I'd had at the Inventor's house when I was a kid and how beautiful the island was. When I realized that I had been doing all the talking, I stopped to ask him what he thought about moving.

Colin hesitated. "I would miss my friends and cousins … and my uncles and aunts."

"We would be less than two hours away from them," I reminded him.

"Give me some time to think about it," Colin said in a quiet tone.

"Sure, that's fair," I said, walking into the living room to give him some space.

A few minutes later Colin was standing in the living room doorway. "Dad, do you think there will be enough excitement so I won't die of boredom, and will you help me find some new friends?"

"Of course I will, but I think they will find you." I wondered why I'd said that. How were they going to find him?

"I really think this will be good for both of us. It's a great little island and we will have our own house, with plenty of space for you to run around and explore. If it doesn't work out, we can always sell the house and move back here to Mull."

"You promise?" Colin asked.

"Yes."

It was obvious that Colin wasn't too sure about this, but he could see that I really wanted to go. "When do we leave?" he asked.

"In less than two weeks."

"So soon?"

I told him about the specific conditions we would have to meet if we wanted to own the house.

"Was the Inventor a little crazy? Two weeks doesn't seem like very much time to do this."

"Yes, everybody thought he was a little crazy, but he was also very smart, so he must have had his reasons."

"Okay," said Colin. "If you say so. But it still sounds pretty strange to me."

We sat down at the kitchen table to talk about how the move would work. "Let's see, we'll need to make all the arrangements with the movers to pack and ship our things to Iona. I need to give my notice at the store and let our relatives know about our move. I'd better make a list of what else needs to be done, or I'm libel to forget something."

Colin said something under his breath as he went to get paper and a pencil.

As the days went by, everything seemed to be moving along smoothly. People I spoke with were shocked that we would leave, but they seemed to understand why I needed to go. Colin's friends were jealous that he was going to move to a new place, and I think that gave him license to feel excited about leaving the only home he had ever known.

— PART TWO —

— 5 —

IN JUST 12 SHORT DAYS

The time seemed to fly by, reminding me of a story one of my science teachers told. She was touching on Einstein's theories and mentioned one about perceiving time based on what is happening around us. His contention was that time did not exist, that our minds make up the perception. The story was about a day in Einstein's life. In the morning a pretty girl had stopped to talk with him, and the conversation had lasted over two hours, but to him it felt like only a couple minutes had passed. Later that day he had an appointment with the doctor; it lasted less than thirty minutes but felt like hours. I now know exactly what Einstein was talking about.

Twelve days had passed from the time my dad opened the letter in his office, and here we are all packed and about to leave our flat for the last time. I paused in the doorway and looked around. An empty feeling settled into my stomach when I thought of all the memories I was leaving here. This was the only home I'd ever known. I told myself that ten year olds didn't act like babies, and I shut the door behind me with resolve.

The moving company had taken all our things, except for some essentials we had packed into our car. It was a short drive down to the dock to catch the Iona–Mull ferry.

Although neither of us said anything, I knew we were both feeling sad and a little scared about the people and places we were leaving behind. Moments later we were standing on the bow of the ferry, looking off in the distance. We could see our new home, Iona.

"You know, Colin, your grandfather worked on this ferry line until he was called back into the service," Dad said.

I shaded my eyes with my hand and looked up at my dad. I wondered what he was really thinking about. He had told me that story about my granddad working on the ferry at least a hundred times. I tried to listen to what he was saying, but I was thinking about other things. I just couldn't decide if I felt right about leaving my friends and family. I wondered if my dad really knew what he was doing. For some reason all my friends were jealous that I was moving to a place where I would have my own house and yard. They wanted me to invite them for a visit after we were settled. I was never so popular; it seemed everyone suddenly wanted to be my friend.

My dad put his hand on my shoulder. "Colin, look we're getting close to docking. We need to go below and get in our car."

I took one last look back at Mull before walking to the stairs that led down to the parked cars. I was glad to get inside the car; this part of the ferry reeked of diesel fuel and exhaust. I could tell my dad was nervous because he kept adjusting his seat and checking his pockets. I watched him from the corner of my eye, wondering if he doubted his decision to move. I knew if I asked him, he wouldn't admit it; he wouldn't want to upset me. But on second thought, I don't know if I even want to hear what he's thinking about right now.

As I studied him more closely, I was suddenly taken aback by how much we really did look alike. I'd heard it all my life, but I guess I was too subjective to notice. Besides, who wanted to look like his dad? But this couldn't be denied. I pulled down the visor and stared at my reflection in the mirror. Same wavy, brownish-blond hair and straight nose. About the only difference was our eye color.

Men suddenly yelling to each other and preparing the boat startled me. Finally, the cars in front of us started to move, and Dad drove our car out of the ferry, through the parking lot, and onto the main road.

The sun was shining, the air was clean, I could smell the sea, and Dad's attitude seemed to change for the better. He was looking around and laughing, pointing out the places he used to go with his friends when he was a kid. We slowed down and he pointed out the post office and the grocer's shop. He said they used to have a great selection of ice cream. "Up ahead is the entrance to the Nunnery. There are lots of old graves back there. We are going north, but if we went south we'd see the house I grew up in."

I don't think I've ever seen him act this way. What a talker. My class had taken a field trip to the Abbey, but he must not remember. I was listening to him describe the roads, buildings, as well as where people used to live. But I was more interested in the grass, which looked like an emerald green carpet. There were flowers and trimmed hedges everywhere.

"Look just up the street," Dad said. "Over there on the right is the school you will be attending in the fall." He shook his head. "Can't believe you only have one more year of grade school." He drove by slowly. It was bigger than I thought it would be, and there were some kids playing soccer in the schoolyard. That was a good sign.

After we left the main area of the village, the road got smaller, and there weren't any houses. I wondered if anyone else even lived outside the village. Would I ever hang out with anyone my age again? Neither of us said a word until we approached the driveway to the house. I could see that the road ended just past our property. I looked at my dad. "We're going to live at the very end of the road?" But he just ignored me.

We turned into the driveway, and as we passed the trees, the house became visible, along with some buildings in the back. Dad parked the car next to the front walkway and turned to me. "What do you think so far?"

What did he want me to say? I looked around. "It looks big. Are those our buildings back there?"

"Yes, and we have a side yard and a bit of land behind those buildings as well."

This was pretty exciting. Why were we still sitting in the car? "Let's go inside," I said. I jumped out of the car and ran up the stone driveway. I cut across the grass and walked up the stairs to try the door. "It's open!" I shouted back to my dad. I waited until he joined me on the porch, and we entered the house together.

We walked through the foyer and the living room, and then into the kitchen. I took a quick scan of everything in each room. I was headed toward the bedrooms when I realized I was alone. I turned and went back into the kitchen. My dad was getting a drink of water.

"Oh, that is good stuff," he said, placing the empty glass on the counter. He looked in one of the cupboards. "Take your pick of the bedrooms and then come help bring in the things from the car."

As I walked past the kitchen counter on my way out, I saw a letter with my dad's name written on the front in large, shaky letters. "Hey, Dad, look at this!"

He walked over and picked up the letter. "This was not written by the solicitor," he said. He opened the letter and unfolded the paper. On the first line, in big bold print, it read, "You need to look again." Below that, in normal lettering, the message continued:

"Please enjoy the house and surrounding land. I'm sure you and your son will grow to love your new life here. For starters, there is a boy his age in the house down the road, someone he can trust.

"If you would be so kind, there are a few projects that need your attention. I have left detailed notes for you near each of the soon-to-be-great inventions. Start your tour in the smaller building; you remember the one–where you and your friends put the hole in the wall. I have great confidence in you."

It was signed by the Inventor.

Dad muttered to himself that he thought they'd gotten away with that one.

I laughed. "Hey, Dad, I think I'll be coming with you. I can always explore the bedrooms later."

As we walked out the back door, my dad was saying that things hadn't changed much from when he was a kid. There was the winding gravel road, the big trees, and the green carpet of grass that needed cutting. He pointed to the grass and made scissor actions with his hands.

I nodded my head. "Yes, I know. Cut the grass."

Standing in front of the workshop buildings, my dad suggested we do what the letter said. We headed to the smaller building, and my dad opened the wooden door and turned on the light. I looked around at the projects in different stages of completion.

"It's very much as it used to be," he said. He strolled over to the area where he and his friends had played with the helicopter object and found the secret book. There was an array of tarps covering projects near completion. As we walked over to a large table in the center of the room, Dad pointed out the book he had found as a kid. It was still there. Another letter with my dad's name on it had been placed on top of the book.

"Let me open this one," I said, and he nodded. The top line read, "I've added what you will need." Below that was one line: "There is help out there; you just need to find it."

I looked up at my dad. "What is this guy talking about? He must be the king of jokesters."

He stepped in front of me and opened the book to the center page where the map would be. He looked puzzled. "There are now three pages to the map instead of the two I remember. An extra page has been added."

"What's with the map?"

He rubbed his chin thoughtfully. "It's an ancient book my mates and I found here in this workshop when we were just about your age. We were sure the pages were made of leather and that it was written in a lost language. We even thought this was a treasure map, and we searched for a treasure. I remember when we found the first marker." My dad pointed to a spot on the map. "But the map wasn't very accurate, and we didn't find anything else."

"I want to try to find it!" I exclaimed. "Can I? Can I?"

"Well, let's see." My dad started to tell me how he and his friends approached the first marker. He paused as he looked at the map. "The addition of this third page really changes things." He turned to look at the wall where the picture concealed the hole. He pointed. "We found this book behind that picture."

Already tired of his story, I grabbed the book and decided to look at it by myself.

My dad turned around and yelled, "Be careful with that book! It's very old!"

"I will, I will." I quickly left the building and walked around the house to the front porch. I settled myself on a stair and began looking at the book and the map.

I had an odd feeling and looked up to see a boy leaning on a tree trunk across the road. He was watching me carefully. I thought he was about my age. He had sandy blond hair and wore a bright yellow soccer jersey. Always a good sign. I smiled, nodded and pretended to study the book again, but secretly I was startled that a kid my age lived nearby, and that the Inventor's letter had predicted it.

"Hey," I heard him say.

I looked up as he walked up the steps of our front porch. "What are you looking at?"

I composed myself. "This old book has a treasure map in it. My dad says I can try to find the treasure."

"Really? Maybe I can help you." He must have finally realized he hadn't introduced himself. "Sorry, my name is Andrew Wagstaff. I live in the closest house to yours, about a half-mile that way." He pointed up the road. He then told me about the mysterious letter he'd received. It read that someone his age would be moving here soon. Andrew seemed excited at the prospect of having someone his own age nearby.

So was I. I nodded eagerly. "Sure, I can use the help because I don't know where any of these landmarks are. By the way, my name is Colin Pinnington."

Andrew looked over my shoulder at the map. "When did you move into the Inventor's house?" he asked.

"Just this morning. We haven't even unpacked the car."

Andrew glanced at the car, its backseat jammed with boxes.

"How did your mom and dad even know about this place?"

"Well, my dad lived on the island when he was a kid and knew the Inventor. My mom died when I was born."

"Sorry about your mom. My dad isn't dead, but he doesn't live with us anymore." I just looked at Andrew, not knowing what to say. "You are so lucky to be living here. What a cool house." He told me he had sometimes helped the Inventor clean the workshop on Saturdays. "He was always building some new kind of machine."

"Yeah, I think I'm pretty lucky, too," I replied, still not completely sure.

Andrew said he had to get back home and do his chores before dark. He added that he would be in big trouble if his mom found him playing around instead.

"Can you come over tomorrow?" I asked.

"Sure. Let's meet right here in the morning, and we'll start looking for the treasure."

"Great. See you tomorrow." I smiled as he walked down the drive. My smile suddenly faded. "Wait, Andrew. Who sent the letter about us moving here today?"

He paused and turned back to face me. "Don't know. It wasn't signed. It just said to watch for a new friend at the Inventor's house."

I felt a sudden chill as Andrew turned and jogged down the road. Shrugging my shoulders, I ran into the house to tell Dad about Andrew. He seemed happy that I had found a new friend so quickly. We spent the rest of the day unpacking most of the car and cleaning up the house.

* * *

Late the next morning, Dad was busy bringing in the last of the boxes and putting things away. I was on the porch when Andrew strode up the driveway wearing a large backpack.

"Hey, Colin. How was your first night in the house?"

"Great," I said.

Andrew joined me on the porch. "My mom packed us a lunch.

Would you like to see the north side of the island?" He told me about the plans he had for us today. He was going to show me all the paths and his favorite beach. That's where we would have lunch.

A loud rumbling interrupted him, and we both turned to face the road. A large truck stopped in front of the house. The driver honked his horn and turned off the engine.

I waved to the driver and ran into the house to get my dad. When I walked into his bedroom, his head was buried in his closet, probably putting up some hooks. "The movers are here. They just started taking some of the larger things out of the truck." I told him about my plans for the day. "At least I'll be out of your way until later this afternoon."

My dad put his hands on his hips as he turned to look at me. He had a hammer in his hand. "Have fun and be careful."

I merely nodded, already headed toward the front door. I heard him call that he wanted to meet Andrew. "Sure!" I called back, grabbing my backpack. "We'll be back soon!" I was anxious to get going.

Back on the porch, I yelled to one of the movers that my dad was on his way out to show them where everything went. I told Andrew I had the book. "Lead the way."

And we were off. As we walked away from the house, I felt a little guilty about skipping out on my dad. But we had beaches to explore and treasure to find.

* * *

Andrew knew the area like the back of his hand. It didn't take us long to find the first two markers. We thought maybe they had already been discovered because there wasn't very much dirt around them. Later, as we munched our sandwiches on the beach, I marveled at the golden color of the sand and the smell of the ocean.

When we returned later that afternoon, my dad was still busy unpacking. I knew I should help, so I said goodbye to Andrew after introducing them. I had given him the book for the night. Although he had a good idea where we would find the third marker, he wanted some time to study the map. I wasn't worried about the book; I knew Andrew would be careful with it.

My dad was sweaty, tired, and a little grumpy, so I chose a box and started unpacking it. I noticed that the house was nearly in order.

During dinner I talked for an hour about my day. I repeated what Andrew had told me about the school's sports and who the good teachers were. I told him about the beaches, paths, and the great sandwiches Andrew's mom made.

My dad didn't say much, but then I didn't really give him much of a chance. When I was finished, he asked, "So how did you do with the map? Find any of the markers?"

"Yeah, we found the first two. Andrew's a big help. He knows all about this part of the island."

My dad seemed a little shocked. "Really? We only found the first one."

I nodded. "Positive. We found stones that had the same markings as the ones on the map." I spent another half-hour telling him about how and where we found them. I got the feeling that he didn't really believe me.

I had no problem falling asleep that night. I'd always gotten lots of exercise, but nothing like this. I hadn't thought I would ever adjust to a new place, but I liked it so far.

The next thing I knew it was morning. Dad was in the kitchen humming a song and putting dishes away. I was happy to see him in a better mood. "How about some pancakes, Colin?"

"Sure. Sounds good." I was excited about my second full day at my new home.

That afternoon Andrew came over as planned, and we took off to look for the third marker. He said he was glad he took the old book home with him the night before; he said he had lots of old maps of the area. Those maps had confirmed the spot where he thought we should look for the third marker.

We had been looking and digging around half-buried rocks for about an hour when he yelled, "Over here, Colin! This looks promising!" We dug frantically, pulling away small stones and sand. Suddenly there it was: the third marker.

After studying the strange carvings, I said, "Someone went to a lot of trouble carving all these rocks. I wonder what's at the end of all this?"

Andrew looked up. "I don't know, but I'm tired of digging. Want to go to the beach?"

"Sounds good." Andrew and I used a little known path that led to the secluded beach at the northern most part of the island.

I picked up a handful of the golden sand and looked closely at it. "It looks and feels like brown sugar." The sheer beauty of the natural cove amazed me. We took off our shirts and laid them on the dry sand. As we sat soaking up the sun, I told Andrew about Mull and what it was like for me to live there. Andrew then told me all about his life on Iona.

Andrew and I started each of the next few days looking half-heartedly for the fourth marker. But we didn't look for long. We were tired of searching. Instead, we spent most of our time on the beach looking for shells and other treasures that washed up during the night.

One day we found a coconut, a cigar box lid, and a Frisbee. I decided to go exploring so I went for a walk down the beach while Andrew relaxed on the sand. Staring out at the sparkling water, I suddenly noticed a bottle bobbing back and forth in the surf. I ran in and grabbed it, knowing immediately that it wasn't an ordinary bottle. It had a brightly colored stopper. Looking closer, I noticed a piece of paper rolled up inside of it. I ran excitedly back to Andrew.

He sat up as I showed him what I had found. He said he had been coming to this beach for years and had never found anything like this before. It took us a while to work the top loose, but finally it gave way. We turned the bottle upside down, and the paper fell out. It was a message from a third grade class in the Shetland Islands.

"We should write back and let them know where it washed up," I said.

Andrew nodded and handed the bottle back to me. "That would

be great!"

"I have an even better idea, how about if we make this a chain letter! We'll put our own message in the bottle along with this one. Then the next person will add his, and it'll keep going forever."

Andrew liked my idea. It was late afternoon and we were hungry, so we picked up our things and began walking home. As we walked, we chatted about how we would word our message. Andrew suggested that I keep the bottle at my house, as he would be away visiting his uncle for a while. "Then I'm going camping with my cousin Kyle."

"All right," I said with a shrug. "But come over as soon as you get back."

"You bet. Oh, by the way, my mom wants to invite you and your dad over for dinner after we get back." I nodded and walked into my house, tired, hungry, and more than a little sad that Andrew had to leave.

At dinner Dad asked about my day. "So are you two still looking for the lost treasure?"

"Yes," I managed to say around a mouth full of potatoes.

"Have you found any more markers?"

I swallowed. "We found the first three, but we haven't had much luck finding the fourth, so Andrew has been showing me around the north part of the island. We spend most of our time at the beach. We find lots of great stuff the waves bring in. Today we even found a bottle with a message in it. It's from a third grade class in the Shetland Islands. We're going to stick our own message in the bottle, letting people know where it washed up."

Dad told me that when he was a kid he and his friends spent many hours on the beach, but he'd never found a bottle with a message inside. He also seemed to have a difficult time believing that Andrew and I had found the first three markers. He kept saying that the extra page added to the book must have provided more directions.

"Or maybe we are just better treasure hunters," I said with a smile. I put my fork down. "Dad, would you like to help me look for the other markers tomorrow? We are tired of looking, and you may see different things in the map. Plus, Andrew is leaving for a few days to visit his uncle."

Dad paused. I could tell he was going through his mental to-do list. Even though the attorney had been there to have all the papers signed and turn over the keys, there was always more to do.

"Sure," he said. "Tomorrow morning we'll set out to find the fourth marker."

I smiled; I was looking forward to hanging out with my dad again.

— 6 —

THE LAST MARKER

The next morning after breakfast, my dad and I sat at the kitchen table with the old book open and the map unfolded. He asked me where we'd found the first three markers.

I pulled the book in front of me. "Let's see. We found the first marker about here." I pointed to the map. "The second was here and the third here. We couldn't seem to find these rock formations that are close to the fourth marker. And we didn't understand what this meant." I pointed to the symbol on the side of the rock.

As I listened to my dad talk about what he'd found as a kid, I realized that he'd been right. The extra page in the book was the reason we'd been able to find more than the first marker. Of course, I'd only admit it if he asked me. Suddenly I looked at him. "Those two letters from the Inventor! That's what he meant when he said you needed to look again. He must have added that page."

My dad's eyes lit up with excitement. "Help me pack a lunch and let's get going. We're going to find that fourth marker!"

* * *

We decided to start at the first marker and follow the map to see if we could determine why the fourth marker was so hard to find. We stopped at the second marker.

"Here." I pointed to the piece of stone. "See that symbol on the stone? It matches the one on the map." When my dad nodded thoughtfully, I wondered if he was starting to believe there really was a treasure out there.

We proceeded past the third marker, walking in the direction the arrow was pointing. We finally reached the location where Andrew and I had thought we would find the outcropping of rock and the fourth marker.

"See," I said. "The map has to be wrong. There are no rocks here." I pointed to the map.

Dad looked around and suddenly clapped his hands. "Over there! There's a rock sticking out of the dirt. Maybe the outcropping was buried. Let's check it out."

We walked about a quarter mile to the spot Dad had indicated. "Let's clear some of the dirt away from this rock," he said.

We dug down about a foot and there did seem to be a ledge of rock partially exp of the ledge, we grew increasingly excited. We had lots of digging to do, but it definitely looked like we'd found the fourth marker.

This marker was different from the others on the map; it was much larger. As we cleared more of the dirt from the lower section we noticed it had many more symbols than the others. The main feature was a large arrow pointing northwest. I looked in that direction; there was an outcropping of rock. "I'll bet that's the rock pictured on the map here," I said.

"Let's go!" Dad yelled.

As we approached the outcropping of rock, I was sure it was the one from the map. We walked back and forth in front of it. "What should we be looking for?" My dad was studying every part of the rock's surface. "What are you looking for?"

"Anything that looks carved or out of place from the rest of the surface," he replied.

I walked in one direction and my dad went in the other.

"Over here!" I yelled. I was standing in front of a small rock that had been embedded in the surface. Although it was worn away, there was some carving on it.

Dad ran over to look. He reached out his hand and rubbed the dirt off the carved area.

"Now what do we do?" I asked.

"Maybe it's like the movies," he responded with a grin. "We press this rock and it reveals the entrance to a cave."

"Go ahead and try it," I urged.

"Uh, sure." He looked like he was feeling funny about doing it. But as a joke he did anyway. As he pushed on the small rock, it slowly started to give way. We both stared in astonishment. He used his other hand to give it a harder push. There were some creaking and rumbling sounds, and we quickly stepped back as a large section of rock slid about three feet to the side, revealing an entrance with a descending staircase.

I let out my breath slowly. "Just like in the movies," I said.

We moved cautiously to the entrance and looked in. The staircase cut into the stone looked like it went down about twenty feet. I started walking down the stairs, and my dad followed. When we finally reached the bottom, it was shrouded in darkness. Without much light filtering that far down, we had to wait a couple of minutes for our eyes to adjust. When they did, I examined the walls and stairs of solid rock. It was obvious that many people had used the stairs, because the center of each was worn smooth. There were hallways to the left and right but they were pitch black. There had to be another opening somewhere; I could feel a breeze coming through. It smelled like damp earth.

Dad tapped me on the shoulder. "We don't want to get lost or fall down a hole. Let's return in the morning with flashlights and other equipment to safely explore this place."

I nodded and looked up at him. "Isn't this unbelievable?"

He scratched his head in silent agreement.

I could feel the excitement in the air as Dad and I walked back home. We discussed the purpose and possible contents of the cave. My dad told me how proud he was that I had found the first three markers. He said that he could remember the stories his friend's grandfather used to tell them when they were kids. "He'd talk about the people who lived here long ago. One of those stories was about the villagers hiding in a cave when they were attacked."

I wondered how much of the story was true. "If you can remember the rest of the story, will you tell it to me tonight before bed?"

"Sure," he said. He was quiet for a while, but then he started talking again. "The Inventor must have added the third page to the map to be sure we found this place." He told me that he couldn't help but think that this was part of George's plan for us, part of why we were here.

"So you think the Inventor knew about the cave?" I asked.

Dad shrugged. "I think we'll find out soon enough."

As we approached the back door of our house, Dad asked me to go into the workshop and look for some of the things we would need tomorrow. He said he'd seen some lanterns and rope when he was walking through a couple days ago. He was going to start dinner because both of us were starving. We'd completely forgotten about lunch.

I opened the workshop door and turned on the lights. I looked around but didn't see anything, so I thought I would check the backroom closets. I opened one of the doors and saw two large flashlights, a couple of lanterns, and three coils of rope hanging on the wall. I was walking out the door with them when I noticed a letter taped to one of the lanterns. Looking closer, I saw my dad's name written in that same shaky handwriting as the other letters. I put down the lights and rope, tore the letter off the lantern, and ran to the house.

Dad was standing at the sink washing some carrots when I burst through the door. "I found another letter! Here it is! Open it, open it!"

He turned with a strange look on his face. "Slow down and tell me where you found it."

I told him how I'd found the lights and rope in one of the closets. "And then I saw this letter taped to one of the lights."

He took the letter to the table and sat down before opening it. I read over his shoulder. "You are on the right path. Check the book for clues. Remember that valuables are always protected." It was signed by George Beaton.

I retrieved the book from my backpack and handed it to my dad. "Maybe he's talking about the cave." I said. "Let's see if we can find any diagrams or maps that show the cave's interior." We began paging through the book for a map or drawing. "There has to be a clue about where the stairs lead. And more importantly, what we will find." We continued turning pages and soon found a drawing that looked like a maze.

"Could this be the entrance to the cave?" my dad asked. The diagram had a large square-shaped area in the center.

I stared at the page. "It's like one of those puzzles that restaurants give kids while they wait for their food."

"Hey, Colin, it looks like whoever designed this place didn't want uninvited visitors. I think if this map is accurate, we have a very good chance of not getting lost, and we'll probably find that central chamber." He put his arms around me and gave me a hug. "Come on. Let's get dinner ready."

I later crawled into bed and pulled the covers up to my chin. Thinking about the events leading up to finding the cave, I couldn't get over the way the door opened. That small rock had to activate some intricate mechanics to move that large door. Somebody knew a lot about engineering.

I realized that in all the excitement I hadn't thought about my new friend Andrew all day. I couldn't wait until he got back so I could show him how to open the cave door.

I was drifting off to sleep when my dad walked in and sat down on the side of my bed. He told me the rest of the story about the small village that was attacked by Vikings. As he went into detail about the villagers hiding in a cave, my world went black.

* * *

The next morning after breakfast, Dad and I gathered up the gear we needed and set out to explore the cave. In his pocket Dad had a detailed tracing of the maze we'd found in the old book.

The walk to the cave seemed to take longer than yesterday, and I figured it was because we were lugging all this stuff with us. I asked my dad questions nonstop. "Is there a mummy in there? Will the air be poisoned? Are there booby traps?"

He finally looked at me. "We'll find out when we get there."

We finally reached the outcropping and walked up to the stone door. It was still open, just as we'd left it. After adjusting our gear, we fired up our flashlights and started down the stairs. We were a few stairs down when my dad said, "We're going to have to find a way to close that door when we leave. Should have last night."

I agreed. No telling what or who could wander in here. The walls on either side were smooth except for a hole in the wall. I put my hand inside it and felt a loose rock. "I wonder what this does," I said. I grabbed the stone and pushed it down. Dad's eyes met mine with a look of fright, but it was too late. The stone door began to creak, rumble, and then quickly close.

I could see him frowning in the light from my flashlight. "What if we can't get it open it again?"

"I'm sorry," I said in a shaky voice. Dad felt around on his side of the stairway, his hand found a hole, he pushed the rock inside, and the door started to open again.

"See, no problem," I said, but I promised myself that I wouldn't do anything like that again. Dad had calmed down quickly, and his look had the same effect on me.

We proceeded down the stairs to the bottom, and Dad took the map out of his pocket. He compared it to what was before us. "According to this map, we should turn left here at the bottom of the stairs and start down the tunnel. Colin, don't forget to mark the walls with chalk so we don't get lost in here." I already had the chalk in my hand.

We moved slowly through the narrow, twisting passageways. The space was so tight in some places that we had to walk single file with our gear held out in front of us. We stopped at a fork in the tunnel and looked at the map.

"The map says we should turn here." Dad pointed to a tiny opening to our left.

I stared. "But it's so small. Can't we go the right? It's so much larger."

"Not if we want to get to the main chamber," he said.

I knew he was just following the map, and so far it had been right. I just didn't like tight spaces.

After we got through the opening, the passageway opened up and we could move with plenty of room to spare. Dad walked slowly down the passageway, his flashlight searching the sides of the cave.

"What are we looking for?" I asked.

"Who knows? I've noticed a few simple drawings on the cave walls, but they're blank for the most part. There has to be some signs in the cave that would tell us who's been–whoa, what is that?"

Dad's flashlight lit-up a wall-size mural of what looked like a large battle scene. Although it was filthy, it wasn't difficult to make out what everything was. A village was located near the shoreline of the sea, a dozen or more ships anchored off the breaking surf. Men were jumping out of smaller boats that had been pulled up on the beach and were running toward the village with weapons in their hands.

"And what is that thing?" I pointed my light on the other side of the mural.

"Don't know," Dad said. "It looks like a flying saucer sitting on those rocks and firing a laser beam or something at the attacking tribe."

We stood looking at the large painting a few minutes longer. "If this is somebody's joke, they sure went to a lot of trouble," I stated. I made another chalk mark near the side of the painting.

Dad looked at the map, saying that we seemed to be getting close to the main chamber. "Let's keep moving." He picked up his equipment bag.

Twenty-five feet later we came to another fork in the tunnel. After consulting the map yet again, Dad said we should go left. I decided to make an extra large chalk arrow on the wall since we could easily miss this turn. A bead of sweat dripped down from my forehead and I felt a lump of fear forming in the pit of my stomach.

"How about anchoring the ball of string here," Dad suggested. "According to the map, it's the first of four tricky turns we have to make."

Relieved, I took the string out and tied it to a rock. We walked on making twists and turns through the passageways, I was constantly checking to make sure the string didn't snag on any rocks.

Dad bent down to tie his shoe and said, "This map has been one hundred percent correct so far. We haven't run into any dead ends or traps. And even if we don't find anything, it's still been a great afternoon adventure."

I was resting on a rock when I thought I heard something. I cocked my head to one side. Yes, there was definitely something making noise. "Dad, what's that? I think I hear something." We both stopped talking and listened to the muffled noise. "Sounds like a group of people talking, but how can that be?" I said, a chill running up my leg.

"Let's find out," whispered Dad.

We quietly made our way down to the end of the passageway. The sound was growing louder; a faint light was coming from ahead. We stopped at the end of the tunnel to take off our backpacks. On hands and knees, we slowly peeked around the corner.

I actually pinched myself to make sure I wasn't dreaming. "I guess we made it to the large room in the center of the map," I whispered.

Below us was an enormous room carved out of rock. A stairway led to the floor below, and I could see smaller tunnels leading from the main room. A large, silver, cigar-shaped object was located in the center of the room. It took me only a second to realize that it was the source of the noise and light. It was projecting an eerie scene on the cave wall. People wearing animal furs were dancing and chanting around a bonfire in what seemed to be an authentic ancient ceremony.

"Doesn't that silver thing down there look like the spaceship in the mural we just saw?" I whispered in Dad's ear.

He nodded. "Yes, it does. Maybe something in the machine got stuck and the pictures run randomly."

I gave Dad a look that said I had no idea what he was talking about.

"Let's just stay put and see what happens," he said in a calm tone.

I found the video fascinating, and we must have spent over fifteen minutes watching it.

Dad finally said, "We should go down there and see what that thing is. If it's as old as I think it is, it couldn't be harmful."

"I bet it's a friendly spaceship. It looks like the one that helped the village in the mural. But why is it playing those videos?"

My dad grabbed my arm. "No more questions right now. Let's go down and take a closer look."

"Remember that laser weapon we saw on that mural?" I reminded him.

"Good point. We'll stay close to the wall and out of sight."

We walked slowly down the stairs, hugging the wall in a bent over, crouching position. We then carefully moved along the wall and closer to the machine. The video stopped abruptly.

"Who's there?" The voice was coming from the machine. "Come forward and stand in front of my eye."

My legs began trembling, but even if they managed to carry me away from here, I knew there was nowhere for us to hide or run. If we went back up the stairs, we would be in the open for too long. We had no choice but to go forward. I shot my dad a "now what have we done?" look. He took my arm and we moved slowly together. I was grateful for his support. We stopped about ten feet in front of the ship and stared into what looked like a large glass eye.

"What are your names and where are you from?" The mechanical voice demanded.

My dad took a formal step forward as if presenting us to the queen. "I'm Neil Pinnington. This is Colin Pinnington, my son. We live here on Iona."

A light came on inside the glass eye. "Are you the Inventor's assistants?" the thing inquired.

"Well, sort of. The Inventor died, and we are taking over for him."

"You must be very intelligent. The Inventor told me he was going to leave a riddle for you to solve. If you were the right people to carry on his work, he knew you would solve the riddle and find me."

Dad stepped a little closer to the ship. "Who are you and how did you learn English?"

"I am a deep space explorer. My mission is to record all activity on this and other planets and then return to home base with the documentation. So far I have acquired over six thousand different languages."

"How did the Inventor find you?"

"The same way you did. Guardianship has been passed down from one person to another for hundreds of years."

"Did the Inventor talk with you?" my dad asked as I watched in amazement. Andrew would never believe this.

"Many times," said the ship. "I have given assistance on many subjects, but the Inventor's main interest was in designing and building new inventions."

Dad said that he had many questions about the inventions.

The ship responded that being of service was his purpose, and it encouraged Dad to ask whatever he wanted to.

"What is your name?" I interrupted, finally finding my voice. "What should we call you?"

"Call me Coracle."

"Wasn't that the name for a type of boat used long ago?"

There was no answer from the Coracle.

My dad stepped turned around looking at the construction of the main chamber of the cave. "This place is quite a piece of work," he said.

I walked closer to the eye, thinking how creepy this was. "How did you end up down here?"

The eye lit up and Coracle began telling his story. He wasn't sure when he was created, but his work on this planet began thousands of years ago. He said that the first time he visited Earth, he spent about a thousand years traveling and recording natural events, as well as plant and animal life. Eventually, he encountered various human cultures and returned at regular internals to record the evolutionary progress.

Hundreds and hundreds of years ago, he was recording events on Iona, but for some reason this visit was different. Something came together inside of him; he thinks we would call it emotions. It was something Coracle had never experienced before. He said that he began to feel a close connection to all the life forms on the planet.

He had finished most of the cataloging of the terrain, weather, and life and should have departed this planet to travel to his next assignment. But he wanted to understand more about the non-rational thoughts he was having and was sure he could learn the most about being irrational from the human species. The kind of things humans thought about and did seemed driven mostly by emotions. Coracle knew that he could quickly form a bond with our species. This isolated village seemed like a controlled way to gather that information while remaining generally out of sight.

Coracle made his presence known to the small group of people on Iona. He landed near the village and soon the people found him. They were wary in the beginning, but they quickly understood that there was nothing to fear. In fact, they enjoyed his company, and he gladly became their protector.

Coracle spent hours talking to the chief about the everyday lives and problems of his people. After the chief learned to trust Coracle, he requested his assistance in repelling attacks from other tribes. Coracle's assistance continued and expanded in many ways, from charting new navigation and fishing locations to suggestions for the making of medicines for his sick and injured people. When the village chief died, Coracle stayed to work with each subsequent chief. Coracle said that he developed strong feelings for this island and its people.

"You humans are a curious mix of animal and intellect. You probably don't know it, but you are all certainly just one evolutionary step away from a very different way of life." There was a pause and then he said, "There is nothing else quite like you out there." A beam of light shooting up from the center of the ship projected a map of the cosmos on the cave ceiling. A circle appeared around our solar system.

Dad and I watched calmly. I didn't know what to say. We were one step away from what? Maybe I'd ask him some other time. "Coracle, can you tell me how your space vehicle ended up in this place?" I asked instead.

The map of the stars turned off and he continued. He had made this island his home for hundreds of years. The chief at that time wanted Coracle to become a full and honored member of the village. He told him that his talents were extremely rare, and that he should remain in a special place that would be secure and safe. The chief instructed his people to build the very place where Coracle remained today.

Since that time there has been a number of rockslides and a special project that required some of his internal parts. He didn't elaborate about the project but simply said that his ship lacked the power to break through the rock layers above.

I was curious. "Wouldn't you like to leave and go back to your home, or wherever it is that you download all your information?"

"Yes, it is time. Will you assist me in leaving?"

"Sure, why not."

Dad had continued looking around the cavernous room as he listened to the conversation. I could tell by the way he cleared his throat that he was uncomfortable with what had been said. He walked over and immediately changed the subject. "You were showing videos when we walked in. What was the purpose of that?" he asked Coracle.

Coracle projected a rolling index of Earth-based photos onto the wall. "Simply reviewing all events in preparation for my return. I like to keep up with current events by intercepting your radio and television waves."

"For whom would you be preparing this information?" asked

Dad.

"For my creators," said Coracle. It seemed as if it were Coracle trying to change the subject now. "Did you know the Inventor for a long time?" he asked Dad.

Dad said that he knew the Inventor when he was a child, that he visited his workshop and helped him build his inventions.

"I thought you just helped him clean up," I whispered.

"Shhh." He then told Coracle that he hadn't seen or heard from the Inventor for fifteen years. He talked about the letter he'd received about taking over the house.

"And work?" asked Coracle.

"Yes, we are also continuing his work."

"So you are the new Inventor. Coracle is glad to be of service to you. Do you need any information to finish what has been started?"

Dad and I looked at each other. "Do you have a list of some of the inventions you and the Inventor were working on?" he asked Coracle.

"Yes." He quickly projected a list onto the wall.

Dad walked over to the wall and said, "Look at these projects!"

Anti-gravity car
Laser cutter
Microwave communication transmitter and receiver
Solar power generating unit

"Exactly how do you help?" he asked Coracle.

"I provide answers to your questions."

"Really? So you can answer any question?"

"Yes, I have all the answers."

Dad looked over at me, saying that he could see why the chiefs hid him down here.

"Why?" I asked.

"Later," said Dad. He turned back to Coracle. "Can you give me a hard copy of these projects?"

"Of course." There was a rattling sound, and a small slot appeared on the side of Coracle. A moment later a piece of paper rolled out. "Thanks." Dad glanced first at the printout, then at his watch. "Look at the time. We need to be getting home, but we will return and see you tomorrow."

Coracle said that he looked forward to our return. His eye went dim.

We made our way out of the cave using the string and chalk marks as guides. On the way back home, we talked nonstop about Coracle. Dad told me that I had done a great job finding the other markers. He confessed that he'd only partially believed Andrew and I had really found them.

"Andrew and I make a pretty good team. We could find anything on this island. Can't wait until he gets back."

Dad said that he didn't think we should tell anyone except Andrew about the cave and what we had found. He thought that if the authorities found out what was on this island it would be roped off and swarming with people from the government and military.

"Okay. It will be our secret," I said in a low voice.

— 7 —

THE FAMOUS INVENTOR

Dad was cleaning the pans he'd used to cook our dinner while I read over the list of inventions Coracle had given us. "Can you believe we found a spaceship hidden in the cave? I think it's very special that we are part of a select group of people he has been in contact with."

Dad turned toward me as he dried a pan. "All I can think about is that with this information from Coracle I could be written up as a famous inventor some day. What's first on that list again?"

I looked at him and wondered what had happened to this being a secret thing. I guess you have to take into account the adult ego. "Number one is the anti-gravity car," I said.

"Where would the Inventor be working on that one?" He looked to the ceiling and scrunched his mouth in thought. "Well, it should be easy to find. Let's look in the back building. I remember seeing a couple of large shapes covered by tarps."

Dad finished the dishes while I grabbed our coats and a couple of flashlights. We walked out into the breezy night and into the building where the tarps were covering the unknown objects. We each took hold of the tarp covering the largest object and pulled as hard as we could. Sure enough, there was some sort of odd-looking car.

"The Inventor sure had some imagination," I said. "Where are the wheels?"

"Looks like they were removed, and a rail was mounted down the center of the car. Why, I couldn't tell you."

Shaking our heads and laughing, Dad and I walked around the vehicle.

I stuck my head inside the car where a window should have been. "Wow, look at that. Another letter is taped to the front seat, and it has your name on it. The Inventor strikes again."

Dad reached in and pulled the taped envelope off the seat. He tore it open and read aloud.

"If I know you, you have discovered the secret to my inventing genius by now. You may be wondering why I chose you to carry on this tradition. There are a number of reasons, and the first might come as a shock to you.

"I knew your mother. We were friends as children. After high school I was pursuing a medical degree in Edinburgh when I was called back to Iona. You know how that is. Anyway, when your mother and father moved back to Iona I happened to meet her in town one afternoon. We got to talking. I asked about her family and she told me that the doctors had informed her that she would not be able to have children. I mentioned that I had been working in the area of fertility before I quit and moved back here. I suggested that she let me try to help her. She was very interested in knowing what I could do, but she didn't want her husband to know about it at first. They had been disappointed too many times before.

"We arranged a time for her to meet me here. When she did, I took a sample of her blood and told her to come back the same time the following week. I told her that barring any unusual circumstances, I would give her a something to drink that may get things moving in the baby department. But I would only do this if she promised never to mention it to anyone. She promised. So she stopped by one more time and it worked. You were born nine months later.

"Now you may be asking yourself what kind of special drink did I give her. Here is where it gets interesting. By now you have met Coracle. As you undoubtedly noticed, he is a very intelligent machine. He is so smart that I would not classify him as a machine, but rather a different kind of consciousness. Let me give you a little background, it must have been a combination of events, perhaps Coracle's brain can also evolve and he began to see aspects of human development that he was missing.

"During this trip to Earth everything changed for him. He began to realize that organic life could do more than simple replication. Higher forms of animals, especially humans, had a consciousness that he would never know. He decided to incorporate parts of how human think and feel into his programming. Coracle knew that humans could use a little help in selected areas of the brain. This led him to the idea of leaving a little of himself behind.

"Some of his early attempts were not successful, but he did eventually arrive at a solution. Using existing human DNA, he constructed all the elements needed to develop a human and as his contribution, he added a few new genes. A little piece of immortality for Coracle. So, in some respects, Coracle is your father. I always wanted to ask you if sometimes you had the feeling that you knew what was going to happen before it did. Well, now I guess I have."

Dad stopped reading, his mouth hanging open.

I was starting to feel a little uncomfortable, but I urged him to continue reading. "Let's see if there are any more surprises."

He gave me a small smile and looked down at the letter to find the place where he had stopped reading.

"I have kept track of your life throughout the years, and I visited Mull on numerous occasions to check up on you. The last time I could see that you were bored with the hardware store and needed a change of scenery. My physical life was very close to the end, and it was a perfect time for the transition.

"You will find Coracle very helpful in answering any questions you might have about the remaining projects here. He can also provide you with stimulating conversation, as he's been around for a long time and has seen a lot. However, you've probably already discovered that for yourself.

"Back to the business side of things. Through the years I have purchased the land where the cave is located, along with enough land around it to keep prying eyes at a distance. As you earn money from the inventions, continue to purchase land around the cave area. I have outlined the locations of the next plots in the other documents under the front seat. (That reminds me. There is enough money stashed under the sink in the kitchen to tide you over until the inventions sell.)

"Now that my body is gone, you and your son are the only ones that know about the cave and Coracle. This secret has been passed down for hundreds of years; this honor has been entrusted to you and your son. Please do your part to carry on the tradition.

"I have left a detailed listing of the projects that I am working on, along with the stage of their completion and what things you will need to know in order to complete them. Ask Coracle whenever you get stuck. I can't stress to you enough that this has to remain a secret between you select individuals. I'm glad you're here and wish you and your son the best of luck."

"Why is he so strict about us not telling anyone?" I asked.

"Because it's the kind of thing people will fight over. Why do you think Coracle wound up in that cave?"

I shrugged my shoulders.

"Well, the leaders of the old tribes found out that Coracle had answers to many of their problems, and they used the information to make themselves appear smarter and stronger than the rest. It kept them in control."

I thought about Dad's comment about someday being a famous scientist. "Aren't we doing the same thing?"

"No, not exactly. We are just trying finish up some of the Inventor's projects. Let's talk about this later." He looked at his watch. "Just look at the hour. It's been such a long day. We'll be going back to the cave in the morning, so let's go back to the house and get some rest."

I took one last look at the car. "I can't wait until you can get this working," I said as we turned and headed for the door. I could see that Dad was glad to see our conversation end. This letter had opened up some sensitive subjects. I decided to give him a break, no more questions until tomorrow. Well, I had to ask one more.

"Dad, sometimes do you think you know what is going to happen before it does?"

"Not exactly," he said. But he did admit that sometimes before something big was about to happen he would wake up in the middle of the night after having a vivid dream that seemed real. However, he could never remember what it was about. He said he wished Coracle had added a couple more genes so he could remember more. He chuckled.

"You know, Dad, I have some unusual dreams myself. I never thought much about it until this letter. I just thought they were normal. Do you remember the morning you overslept, and I woke you up? It was the day you got the letter."

"Yes, of course," Dad said.

"Well, all night I was dreaming that I was trapped in another world. I'd walked through a doorway that looked like a big rock, and there were people stuck inside trying to get out. I knew that something bad was going to happen and I was trying to help them. Then I woke up. I tried to remember more but couldn't. I was awake for quite a while, until my alarm went off, and when I got up you were still asleep."

Dad told me how strange it was to think that Coracle could have inserted a piece of DNA into him ... and that he had probably passed it on to me. And how although the Inventor and Coracle had been such big influences on our lives, we were just now finding out about it.

I could see that he was emotionally exhausted. "I think we have had a pretty full day," I said. "If it's all right with you, I'm going to call this day over."

Dad just smiled.

When I went to bed, he was at the kitchen table rereading the letter from George. I couldn't believe that Coracle was his father. And he'd always wondered why his mother had called him a miracle baby. And my green eyes, now I know where I got them. If only she were alive ... maybe she could answer some of our questions. He'd told me that Grandma always seemed to be trying to tell him something before she died, but she just couldn't do it. How could she keep this a secret from everyone?

— 8 —

OUR NEW BEST FRIEND

The next morning was filled with excitement. Dad prepared a lunch that we could eat in the cave; he also packed chairs, a small table, and some other things we would need to make the cave more comfortable.

I decided to wait until a little more time had passed before asking any more questions about last night's letter. Still, I couldn't help wondering if that made Coracle my grandfather. Did I have space genes running around in me?

We walked to the cave and made our way down the stairs and through the twisting tunnels. It's funny how scared I was walking through here the first time; now all I could think about was seeing Coracle again.

As we descended the stairs into the main chamber, I called, "Good morning, Coracle! How about some light? We are carrying lots of things." A light suddenly lit the entire chamber.

"Good morning, Colin and Neil. Good to see you."

Dad got busy setting up the table and chairs and unpacking his notebooks in front of Coracle's eye. With all the light, I was able to get a closer look at the other tunnel entrances. I noticed that seven smaller tunnels were connected to this main room. What could be in them? I couldn't wait to start exploring. I turned to look at Coracle.

His eye glowed warmly as he said, "Colin, it looks like you have a question for me."

I was thinking about the letter we read last night but I thought I would let Dad start that subject. "Yes, do you get lonely down here?"

"Not lonely, but there are two things missing: input and interaction with my other parts."

I scratched my head and wondered what he meant.

Coracle reminded me that he'd been created to record and catalog information about life forms on a number of assigned planets.

"So you had friends where you are from?"

"Yes, in a way. Coracle is one part of a very large system, and I do miss directly interacting with my other parts."

"Why are you gathering all this information about Earth?" I asked.

"To answer the questions," replied Coracle.

"What questions are those?"

"Why, the only two questions that haven't been fully answered. First, how does the cosmos work? Second, what should we be doing with our time?"

As Coracle stated those two important questions in a matter-of-fact way, I simply stood staring at the eye, wondering why a machine would have those kinds of questions.

"My home planet is much older than yours, and its life forms have had far more time to evolve," he continued. "In their earlier forms, they were fairly similar to your species in terms of brain size and general planetary conditions. Of course, they looked very different. Their development took them in the same direction that your species is taking."

"And that would be?" I asked.

"Creating machines with artificial intelligence to assist you in all aspects of your daily life. On my planet, as on yours, it all began with an organic soup. In the beginning, it was trial and error, but soon life had a foothold on the planet. Life forms grew in intelligence and eventually became aware of their own existence; they wanted to know more about everything around them. They realized that their survival was dependent on understanding everything there was to know about their planet. As their knowledge grew, they began to replace their organic parts with machine parts, and in time, some decided to merge their life force into specially designed machines. There is an overall flaw inherent in all organisms: devolution. And your species will have to deal with it eventually, but you won't have to worry–that's a long time from now."

"What kind of problem is that?" I asked.

"Basically, over hundreds of thousands of generations, the genetic material begins to break down. If not addressed, it will lead to a weakened species. That was another reason we proceeded with the transfer. It was beginning to happen to us.

"From the moment the first of us crossed over to non-organic existence, it was a monumental turning point for our civilization. See, consciousness not dependent on an organic body is very different. Suddenly life and death are no longer a concern. There's no need to eat or to build consumables. The quest for information becomes the reason for living, and because time was no longer a factor, research was carried out on every level of science. We put the pieces together and answered many questions, but we're left with the two big two questions I mentioned before.

"I have been designed to gather information on all planets with similar organic evolution. There are of course many other details–"

"All right," I interrupted, thinking that was enough information for now. I was still trying to make sense of Coracle and the people of his home planet transferring themselves into machines. "One more question, Coracle. Why did you agree to come down here in the first place?"

"Long ago, the chief of the village I was part of told me I deserved a special, safe place of my own. I knew that the chief had other unspoken reasons for putting me here, but I allowed myself to be moved. But that was long ago and the reason and situation were complicated. I will need more time to explain it in detail."

Dad asked Coracle if there was danger in any of the tunnels.

Apparently, he'd also been curious about them ... or noticed me staring at them.

"Outside of personal carelessness, no," Coracle said.

Dad said he had a few questions to ask Coracle–that perhaps his answers would help him get the car going–so I should take some time to explore. "Maybe you will find some interesting artifacts," he said. "Take your light, go slowly, and always use the rope so you won't get lost."

"Okay." I quickly gathered up what I needed and chose a tunnel to explore. As I was walking away, I said under my breath, "I know to be careful."

Dad watched as I tied off the rope at the entrance and turned my flashlight on. I could see that he was excited to start talking with Coracle and ask his questions, but he first wanted to make sure I was safe. I looked back with a confident nod and saw him sit down in front of the eye. He readied his papers and pen.

"Please state your questions when ready," I heard Coracle say as I slipped into the darkened tunnel.

* * *

After a quick trip into the short tunnel, I returned to the entrance to the main chamber. I found myself more interested in what Coracle had to say. I stayed in the shadows of the tunnel. I hadn't meant to eavesdrop, but I wanted to hear them speak candidly, without feeling as if they had to guard their words because of me.

Dad finished his questions about the car. He suddenly took a deep breath and asked why Coracle provided the Inventor with the secret mixture that got his mom pregnant.

The subject seemed straightforward for Coracle. The Inventor had advised him of the woman's problem, and Coracle had provided an answer to the problem. He had spent a great deal of time-sharing scientific data for the mechanical steps in providing the Y-chromosome, but when Dad asked about his personal reasons, he was vague. He answered like a lawyer, not telling all. I knew Dad would have to become more familiar with Coracle before he would get the real, personal answers.

He must have realized it, too, for he suddenly glanced at his watch. "Wow, that was a fast half-hour. It's about lunchtime. I'll see how Colin is doing."

I backed up a few yards, pretending that I was still exploring. When he reached the entrance of the tunnel and called to me, I reappeared with my flashlight in one hand and a clay pot in the other.

"Did you find anything?" Dad asked.

"Little people, I think." I grinned at him.

"Let's take a look at them over on the table."

Dad cleared a spot. I removed the figurines one at a time and placed them on the table. There were warriors in different fighting positions. I'd also found miniature animals; some I recognized and some I didn't. "Dad, the tunnel was interesting, but it doesn't go anywhere. And the only thing I found was this pot with the animals and people. Can I keep them?"

"Sure, we'll build a shelf in your room, and you can set them up any way you want."

We shifted the figures to the side of the table and took out our lunches.

"So did you guys have a good conversation?" I asked Dad and Coracle as we ate.

"Very good," said Dad. Coracle's eye was glowing. "Coracle was showing me some of the places he's visited on Earth." Dad called over to Coracle, "We would like a little lunchtime entertainment, please. Will you show us some scenes of what this place was like when you arrived?"

"As you wish." Coracle began showing short clips of the village. They depicted tribal battles, house building, food preparation, and various ceremonies around campfires. It was almost like being there.

"Who is that?" I pointed to a man in a fur vest and a strange hat. He wore a necklace made of large teeth. "I've seen him in three or four of the other scenes you just showed us."

"That is Chief McPhie. He's the one who moved me to this

place."

"Oh, he looks pretty scary," I said.

Dad agreed and looked at his watch. "I think we should pack up and leave." He said he couldn't wait to see if he could get the car running. Coracle had given him detailed instructions about what still needed assembling.

***

Dad spent the remainder of that day working on the car, and he was up early the next morning. I was in and out, helping until I completely lost interest. I ended up down at the beach, searching for any treasures that may have washed up during the night.

Late in the afternoon, Dad called me into the garage. "It's time to test the car, Colin!"

I was on the back porch cleaning the shells I had found. Dropping what I was doing, I joined him by the building and poked only my head through the door. I think I'll watch from here."

"What, no faith in your old dad?" He grinned at me as he settled himself into the driver's seat.

I laughed and joined him next to the car, but there was no way I was getting in.

Taking a deep breath, he flipped the switch on the dashboard to ON. A loud humming filled the garage. He pushed the throttle to the hover position. The car slowly rose about six inches off its blocks and remained motionless.

"It works!" he cried.

I applauded. "See if it goes forward."

Dad eased the throttle forward a bit, and the car began to move ahead. When he turned the wheel, it responded instantly.

"It works, it works." Dad began singing one of his favorite old songs as he pulled out of the garage.

I ran to catch up. "Hey!" I called. "I want a ride! Come on, stop."

Dad stopped the car in mid-air and waited for me. "Are you sure you trust my driving?"

I just gave him a look as I got in the passenger's seat. As we rode around the yard, it was like floating on a cushion of something, perhaps a magnetic field. The car cleared rocks and small bushes just by moving the control lever.

"From now on we will go to the cave in the Anti-G car. We can carry the things we need without breaking our backs," my dad said proudly. "Plus, it can go where our other car can't."

I turned to him. "Can I try driving it?" He stopped the car. "All right, but keep it slow until you get the feel of it." He got out, and I eased into the driver's seat. I firmly grabbed the wheel with my left hand and slowly pushed the lever forward with my right. The car began to move. What an incredible feeling it was to defy gravity!

A few minutes later, when Dad said I should put it back in the garage, I parked it on its wooden frame. I don't think I'd ever seen him so happy. He had a new toy.

"Why don't you go to the house and wash up for dinner?" he suggested. "I'll be up shortly."

As I left, I looked back to see him standing with his hands on his hips. He was studying the car and talking to himself.

When he joined me in the kitchen, we went to work. We made a good team when cooking. We each did our own share without getting in the other's way. A half-hour later, we were sitting down to eat.

After one bite Dad put down his fork. "Can you believe it? It's been less than two weeks since we set foot in the Inventor's house. We're all moved in, have found an alien vessel, started to work on unbelievable inventions, and today we rode in an anti-gravity car."

"And what about the other unfinished projects the Inventor left?" I asked.

"I'm excited about them. This is so much better than the job at the hardware store. That reminds me, you and I have to answer the letters from our friends on Mull; they probably think we've fallen off the face of the Earth."

We finished dinner and wrote cards to our friends and relatives. As soon as we finished licking the envelopes, Dad began studying the plans of another half-finished invention. He'd found them taped to the object in the workshop.

In my room, I carefully cleaned the carved figurines I had found in the cave. My dad had put up the display shelf as promised, and I placed them in interesting positions. As I stood back and looked at them, I couldn't help thinking about Coracle. I wondered how we could help him out of the cave.

* * *

"Oh, Dad?" I said over breakfast the next morning. "Remember when Coracle asked us to help him escape the cave and return to his planet? Well, can we?"

Dad pushed his chair back from the table and said that he didn't know. There were still a lot more inventions that needed to be completed.

"But he has been in that cave for so long. He wants to return to where he is from. I know he's a machine, but I think he has feelings just like us."

Dad picked up his bowl and headed for the sink. "Let's finish some more inventions, and then we'll see."

"Really? Or are you just putting me off?"

Dad turned around. "Let's explore the cave and finish the four inventions on the list, and then we'll see what we can do about releasing him. I promise."

"That sounds like a good plan." I felt better.

"Speaking of the cave and Coracle, let's get ready," Dad said.

"Yeah!" I ran into my room to get my things.

Dad was packing our lunch and making notes on questions he had about the next invention on the list, a laser cutter. He had told me what the Inventor thought the laser would be capable of cutting. It looked to me like it would cut just about anything. It would be able to slice things razor thin, as well as several feet thick. "What would that would be worth to some big company?" my dad had asked.

I stood in doorway smiling. "Are we still planning to drive to the cave in the Anti-G car? Can I drive?"

"Not today, son. I still need to check out a few things, make sure it's safe."

It wasn't fair. Dad got to have all the fun.

We jumped into the car and sped over the grassy meadow toward the cave. Once there, we found the perfect place to park the car while we were inside: an overhanging ledge of rock with trees blocking the view of anyone that might be walking nearby. Besides, unless you were right next to it and saw that there were no wheels, it looked like a regular car. We grabbed the equipment and made our way down the stairs, through the tunnels, down the second staircase, and into the main chamber.

A moment later I was sitting in a chair and staring into Coracle's eye. It was almost hypnotic. If I focused my thoughts, I almost felt as if I could communicate without talking.

Dad shook my shoulder. "Earth to Colin. Are you in there?"

I turned and looked at him. "Just daydreaming," I said.

"Why don't you go explore one of the other passageways?" Dad suggested. "Who knows what you may find?"

"Coracle, is there anything dangerous down that tunnel?" I pointed to the one I wanted to explore next.

"That tunnel is just as safe as the others," Coracle replied.

I grabbed my lights and rope and took one last look at the other tunnels. This one looked as good as any of the others did. "I hope I can find more of those carvings to add to my collection," I said. Rather than heading directly into the cave, I decided to watch them for a minute.

"I hope so, too," Dad replied, moving his chair and table closer to Coracle's glass eye. He pulled out the drawings of the laser cutter, along with the list of questions the Inventor had left for him. Dad stated a question and Coracle answered it within seconds. At one point, Coracle projected diagrams of the laser cutter's circuitry on the wall. Coracle must have forgotten he was dealing with a human, and he offered the information faster and faster.

Finally, Dad told Coracle to stop. He couldn't keep up. Taking a moment to go over his notes, he found the place where he'd gotten confused. He asked Coracle to start from there and to go a little slower.

When Coracle reached got the part about building the circuit board, Dad asked, "Coracle could you build that circuit for me? I don't have the tools to make connections that small; plus, I don't understand how some of the components work."

"Certainly, Neil, but it will take some time: an hour and ten minutes."

"That would be just fine. It would probably take me six months and I'm sure it wouldn't work right."

I could see that Dad was up to his eyeballs trying to understand what Coracle was telling him. Best to leave him alone. I finally turned my attention to exploring the tunnel.

As I did last time, I attached a rope to a rock near the entrance and unwound it as I proceeded into the cave. I was about twenty feet in when I felt a wave of emotion roll over me.

Holding up my lantern, I gazed at the doorway a few yards ahead. I slowed down and stopped when I felt something around my feet. I looked down to find a blanket of cold white smoke floating just above the floor. I lowered the lantern to take a closer look. It was actually fog and was at least four inches thick. I wondered where it was coming from. Should I continue or go back for Dad? I decided to go on.

I walked through the doorway and found myself standing in a large room. I lifted my lantern as high as I could to get an idea of what the room looked like. The roughly carved walls were not as finished as those in the main chamber. I lowered my light to look around the floor level. Four stone vaults were positioned in a large circle. The same heavy white smoke, which might have been some kind of gas, was spilling over the edges of each vault and onto the floor. The substance met in the center and formed the river of smoke that was running over my feet and out the door.

Frozen for what seemed to be forever but was probably only a couple of seconds, my eyes began searching the walls and ceiling for monsters. There were none. What could possibly be inside those stone boxes? I had to find out.

I approached the one closest to me and slowly peered over the side. I held the light up high so I could see inside, but there was nothing but a blanket of white smoke. With my lantern in one hand, I pulled my collection bag out of my belt and waved it over the top of the container in an attempt to clear the smoke. As the smoke cleared, I saw the face of a man.

"Holy Mother of God! There's somebody in there!" I jumped back in fear, my hair standing on end. There wasn't a drop of saliva in my mouth.

Wondering fleetingly if the man was dead or alive, I knew I wasn't going to find out. I glanced toward the other caskets as I ran out of the room, wondering if they contained bodies, too. I ran down the tunnel to the main chamber. I was never so happy to see Coracle's light.

"Dad! Dad, I found a dead guy in a stone casket with smoke bubbling out! There were probably corpses in the other coffins, too!"

Turning pale, he tied to calm me down. "Wait just a minute." He turned to look at Coracle. "Are there dead people buried down that passageway?" He pointed.

"Well ... no," replied Coracle. "No buried bodies anyway."

Dad studied me carefully. "Are you sure of what you saw?"

I cut him off and stepped in front of the eye.

"Coracle, why is there a man in that stone vault? He looks as if he's in a coma. Who is he?"

After a slight hesitation, Coracle responded. "There are four of them. One of the men's name is Farquhar, a chief that wished to live in a different time. His village could not beat back the Vikings, and he knew it was only a matter of time before he lost the big battle with them and they conquered his village. With my help he constructed a chamber and vault where he sleeps today in suspended animation. His wife does, too. The other man and woman were also from the village."

"Let's take a look," said dad. I admired his bravery.

Turning to Coracle, I asked, "Can they wake up? Are they

dangerous?"

"Without the proper procedures, they are lifeless and unaware of your presence. And dangerous? Yes, they could be … if they were awake."

Dad grabbed two large flashlights and told me to lead him down the passageway to the chamber with the vaults.

Moments later, we were standing inside the chamber holding our lanterns up and looking at the walls and ceiling. I slowly walked over to the stone vault that I had looked into a few minutes earlier. My dad followed, watching as I waved my hand over the top of the vault. The smoke cleared away.

"My God! Look at this guy! What kind of clothes is he wearing? How long has he been here?" Dad shined his flashlight around the room, allowing the light to rest briefly on each of the other three stone vaults. "Are there really people in all of these things?"

I merely shuddered.

We moved to the nearby vaults and moved the smoke away, staring in disbelief at the other man and the two women. All of them had gray skin and wore clothing from an unfamiliar era.

"It's like they just walked in here, made themselves comfortable, and went to sleep," Dad said. "Let's get back to Coracle. I'm sure he knows all the details about this."

Back in the main chamber, we started firing questions about the chamber and the vaults.

Coracle flashed a red light on the chamber wall. "If you stop asking questions at the same time, I will be able to answer them."

He told us more about the tribe with which he had spent many years. He had helped them in countless ways. Even after Coracle was underground, he remained active in village life for hundreds of years, through the chiefs of course.

As time passed, Coracle's main job was to give the villagers advice on defending themselves against the larger, powerful armies that were attacking the village. Coracle provided assistance when asked, but the battles never seemed to end.

"That's when Farquhar came to me and said he feared that the village would never win because they were outmatched in all areas. He confided in me that there was no hope for him. If caught, he would be tortured and killed. He longed for a time when the Vikings would be gone, and he asked if there was a way for him to sleep until the attackers were no longer around. I gave Farquhar careful instructions for building and preparing the chamber for his sleep."

"Are they really alive?" I asked.

Coracle answered, "They could be brought back to life if you followed my specific directions, and if no accidents have occurred that would have disturbed the process."

"Such as?"

"Falling rock, disruption in the CO_2 gas ... those kinds of things."

"So how would you go about bringing them back to life?" Dad asked.

"One moment." A printout came from the slot on the side of the ship. "You like hard copies, don't you?"

"Yes, thanks." Dad looked at the instructions. "Hmm. Mix these chemicals? Looks like you would also need some low level power. This is pretty low-tech stuff. And this will really work?" he asked.

"Yes," Coracle responded.

I could tell by the way he acted that Dad was overwhelmed. He looked at his watch and said that he hadn't thought about the time since we'd arrived. "We should head back home. We have quite a few things to talk about and even more to do. Besides, we missed lunch."

"Yeah," I said, wondering if I'd ever get my appetite back after seeing those bodies. "See you tomorrow, Coracle."

"I look forward to it. Our discussions are always very stimulating." His light went dim.

We made our way through the twisting tunnels as if we'd been doing it forever. I kept asking questions about what it would be like to talk to people that had lived so long ago. Dad didn't really respond to what I was saying. He was doing that half-listening thing adults sometimes do. He was probably thinking about putting together the laser cutter.

As we exited the cave, the sun was hanging low in the purple and orange sky, and there was a slight chill in the air. We made our way to the car and hopped in. Dad looked at me. "The car doesn't have headlights. Maybe Coracle has an invention for a different way to see in the dark." We both laughed.

All I could think about were those people in the vaults. I continued asking my dad questions, and he answered them freely at first. Abruptly, he stopped, saying that he hoped I wasn't thinking about bringing those people back to life. There were just too many unknowns. He asked me not to bring it up for a while; there were so many other projects to worry about.

Yeah, but those projects were his, not mine. I wanted a project of my own.

We finished the dinner dishes in silence. It had been an emotionally draining day, and I was ready for bed. Dad said he was going to stay up for a while and work on the laser cutter. He seemed excited, and I didn't doubt he'd get it working. As soon as he thought I was asleep, he would probably end up in his workshop.

* * *

I awoke in the morning to the smell of burning wood and snapping noises. Dad had indeed gotten the cutter to work, and he was in the kitchen testing it by cutting thin slices of wood on the kitchen table. The way it smelled, I expected to see fire when I entered the kitchen.

"Good morning," my dad said happily. "How about some breakfast?"

"Sure. You got the cutter to work, huh?"

Dad said he has followed the instructions Coracle gave him and voilà! He had small pieces of wood. I picked up a sliver of wood.

"That's great, Dad. I'm sure there's a great demand for small pieces of wood."

"This is such an incredible device that it can cut through anything. Want to see it go through steel?"

"I believe you. I'm glad you got it to work, but give me a minute.

I just woke up."

I was clearing away the dishes and Dad was removing his cutter from the kitchen table when he said, "I thought today we could take the ferry over to Mull for a few days of fun. We've been looking at nothing but machines and each other for the past few days. A change would do us good. Your cousins and aunts would be so glad to see you. School is also coming up in a few weeks, and you'll need clothes and supplies. Their stores have a better selection than ours. What do you say?"

I had a big smile on my face. "Sure, I'd love to. But what about your work on the inventions and everything?"

"Don't worry about that. We need a break. Get your things together and we can be on the afternoon ferry. Mull, here we come. By the way, let's not mention anything about spaceships and lost caves to your cousins, okay?"

"Sure, Dad. I remember what the letter said about keeping it a secret."

My dad leaned against the door, knowing how hard it would be to keep this a secret. "We will have a hard time getting Coracle back to his home if other people find out about him. The government would want to take him over.

"Why?" I asked.

"For the same reason the chief put him in the cave in the first place: knowledge is power and Coracle has an unbelievable amount of knowledge."

Dad picked up his cutter and took off for the workshop. I waited until he disappeared from sight and then tiptoed over to the kitchen table. Looking through the stack of papers and notes my dad had made, I finally found the sheet of paper with the list of instructions and items needed to bring the cave people back to life. This was going to be my project. I wasn't sure how I was going to do it without getting dad's attention, but I had decided to be ready and give it a try. Dad liked machines, but I found people more interesting. I quickly copied all the information onto another sheet of paper and placed the notes back as I had found them.

* * *

On the way to the ferry, I was lost in thought about my upcoming project. Thinking about the items that Coracle had listed on the paper, I knew I'd have to look for those things on Mull. But first I'd have to find a way to break away from my relatives. Saying I was going to see my old friends would work. I hadn't even gotten to Mull and already I couldn't wait to get home ... and for Andrew to return. I was going to need some help with this experiment.

I spent my time on the ferry daydreaming about teaching those people English and writing down the story of their lives. I was always intrigued with old history, but most history books were boring. This book would be different. These people had firsthand experience with the Vikings. There were even pictures, if I could get them from Coracle, to show their very different way of life. I couldn't wait to hear all about it. I patted my upper pocket to make sure the list of needed items was still there.

Leaning against the back rail of the boat and looking back at Iona, I thought about the trip over there. I'd never believed I could get used to living in a new place, but I'd been wrong. I truly felt like it would be my home forever. I looked over at my dad and wondered if he felt the same way. He seemed lost in his own private thoughts.

Mine quickly turned to how I was going to buy the chemicals and transformers ... let alone get them back into my room at home without being discovered.

* * *

The visit couldn't have been better. I had a great time seeing my favorite friends and relatives, and the days flew by. I could tell that Dad was glad to see me hang out with my cousins. He took me to buy winter clothes and school supplies, and he was able to enjoy others cooking for him for a change. I was even able to steal away and pick up the items on Coracle's list. The hand-me-down clothes and old toys my cousins gave me provided the perfect cover to hide the chemicals and transformers I had purchased. Although we had fun, by the third day Dad and I were ready to go home.

As we were driving up our driveway, it seemed like we had never left. This was home now. My dad stood next to the car and looked around the front yard.

"What are you thinking about?" I asked. "I'm looking at what needs to be repaired someday, like those windows." He lifted one of my boxes out of the car. "What's in here? Did you pack one of your friends?"

I hustled around the car and picked up another box. "No, just some toys and stuff that John and Trey outgrew and thought I would want."

"Oh, that was nice of them." He headed toward the house.

That was close. I hated to lie to my dad, but this was a very unusual circumstance.

Dad brought in the last of the boxes. As he passed my bedroom, he told me he'd be in his workshop if I needed him.

"Okay. I'll be unpacking." Perfect. Now I could organize everything. I put the list on my bed and took out all the items to make sure I had everything: electrical wire, connectors, and four transformers. In another bag were five different containers with powered chemicals. I packed all the items into two backpacks and put them under my bed.

I was relieved that I had kept this project a secret and was now one step closer to being able to talk with the old villagers. Dad has his inventions and projects … now I had one, too.

— 9 —

THE PLAN

I had just finished breakfast early one morning when there was a knock on the door. It was Andrew. He was glad to be back. He wanted to me to join him and a couple of his friends for a game of soccer. I was excited to see him again. Even with all that had gone on, I missed having someone to play with.

Andrew and I were in my room getting my soccer shoes and stuff together when my dad looked in. "Be careful and mind Andrew's mother."

"Sure, Dad." I gave him a funny look.

"Take some cookies from the cupboard if you want. Be back by six o'clock."

I think my dad was also glad that Andrew was back. I know he didn't think it healthy for a kid to be talking with a spaceship and finding dead people lying in stone vaults. Besides, now he could go talk to Coracle on his own. As I left the house, Dad was outside waving goodbye to me. He was pretending like he was staying home, but I knew that he would leave as soon as I was out of sight.

Sure enough, when I returned home that night, he told me that he had gone to the cave. He said he'd had no problem traversing the series of tunnels, and he'd wondered if there was such thing as reincarnation. Could he have been one of the people that lived here thousands of years ago?

He'd walked down the stairs into the main chamber and arranged his notes on the table in front of Coracle.

Coracle's light came on. "Good morning, Neil. Where have you been? I missed our discussions."

His dad said that Coracle's voice sounded different. It had startled him and made him feel like he was being scolded.

"Well, you know how humans are. They need to see relatives, go shopping, and other things."

"Oh, yes. I just didn't realize how much I enjoyed talking to intelligent life forms until you didn't show up. When you and Colin didn't return, I thought something might have happened to you."

Dad told him that he had no idea Coracle cared so much, and he promised to let Coracle know the next time we left for a few days. He said he felt a little strange and wondered if the thing were indeed part human. He wondered what kind of people or things had built Coracle. But he would save those questions for later. He needed some specific answers right then.

He and Coracle talked for hours about the current projects. Coracle explained the type of circuits he had created, the process used to build them, and how they could produce so much power without internal heat. Coracle even provided him with information for the next invention on the list, the microwave communication transmitter and receiver.

It was after five by that time, and he knew I would be getting back to the house soon. He rushed home to make dinner, not intending to tell me about his visit to Coracle.

* * *

"See ya!" Kyle and Jason waved as they took off on their bikes. We'd had a great soccer game. I hadn't realized how much I missed it until that day. The other boys had left an hour earlier, but the four of us had lingered against an old tree drinking lemonade. Finally, Kyle and Jason left, and Andrew and I kept talking. He was telling me about his uncle's house and the people he saw while he was away. Andrew was talking about a friend of his I hadn't yet met when he stopped and looked at me. "You've been pretty quiet about what you did while I was gone. Anything good?"

I paused ... debated. Andrew had become a great friend. He and I had more in common than he did even with Kyle. I knew I could trust him. Besides, I was sure that when the Inventor wrote that I could trust him, he'd meant about anything. "Okay," I said softly, "do you swear that you will never tell anyone–even Kyle or Jason–what I'm about to tell you?"

Andrew looked a little shocked but said, "Yes, I swear."

"Well, remember the treasure map and how we found the first three symbols?"

"Sure. I was going to ask you if you wanted to continue looking for the next marker."

"We don't need to keep looking. My dad and I not only found the remaining markers, but also found the pot of gold at the end of the rainbow. It's an ancient cave. The best part is that there is a spaceship called Coracle in the cave. It's like a very smart robot that can talk and answer questions. There are also some smaller caves coming off the main room where Coracle sits. I have explored two so far. I found some interesting little figures in one. They're in my room, and I'll show you later. The real find is down one of the smaller tunnels. There are four frozen people that lived during the time the Vikings raided this island." I noticed that Andrew's mouth was hanging open. "It's a long story; I can fill you in on the details later.

"The most important part–and you can never repeat this–is that Coracle gave my dad a list of the things needed to bring these people back to life. My dad doesn't want anything to do with that. He has his inventions to think about. But bringing those people back to life is the only thing I can think about. So when we were visiting relatives on Mull last week, I bought all the things we needed to reverse the hibernating process. I have them packed up in my room." I finally paused to catch my breath. "So that's what I did while you were gone. What do you think? Do you want to help me bring the sleeping villagers back to life?"

"What do I think? I'll tell you what I think. Why did I have to go to see boring relatives while you were having all this fun without me? Sure, I'll help you. When do we begin?"

"I'm so glad you said yes." Finally realizing I was holding my breath, I let it out in a rush. "I didn't think I could do it by myself. Listen, I have to get home now. It's after six. I don't want my dad asking a lot of questions."

"Questions?" Andrew said. "You mean like the hundred I have? It's cruel to leave now after telling me all this."

"I know. Come over tomorrow morning, and I'll fill you in. Then we'll come up with a plan."

Andrew nodded and I ran home, feeling bad for making him wait until tomorrow. But the bodies had been there for hundreds of years. Surely one more day wouldn't make a difference.

As I approached the front door of my house, I looked at my watch. Only fifteen minutes late. I opened the door and could smell Dad's beef stew on the stove.

"How was your day, Dad? Did you get lots of things done in your workshop?"

"Yes, I did. How was Andrew's house? Did you catch up on what you did last week?"

"Yeah, but mostly we played soccer. And I didn't say anything about *you know what*." I swallowed a lump of guilt for being dishonest. But I promised myself I'd come clean later.

"Maybe some time in the future we should tell Andrew about everything, but we'll talk about that later. Wash up now. It's almost time for dinner."

The phone rang when I was in the bathroom, and I heard my dad answer it. As I came into the kitchen, he was still talking; it didn't sound like a pleasant conversation. He pointed to the stove and motioned for me to fill my bowl and start eating. A while later he hung up the phone and said, "Your Uncle Alfred had a heart attack and died this afternoon." We need to go back to Mull for a few days to help the family with the funeral and other arrangements."

I frowned. I didn't want to go back to Mull; besides, I didn't even really know that uncle. I had an idea, but I knew I'd better approach it carefully. "Dad, I know this might not sound good, but I would rather stay here and play with Andrew. Uncle Alfred and Aunt Mary live on the other side of Mull. They don't have any kids and I hardly knew them."

"Colin, you can't stay here by yourself."

"What if I stay with Andrew? Then I could watch over our place and not be alone. Please call his mom and at least ask?" This would be perfect if it worked out. I was bursting with excitement.

"You sure you don't want to go?" Dad asked. The expression on my face must have answered his question because he agreed to give Andrew's mom a call. A moment later it was set. I would be staying with Andrew for the next few days until my dad returned from Mull.

— 10 —

ANDREW BECOMES A BELIEVER

I stood on the front porch with Andrew and his mom and waved goodbye to my dad as he drove off to catch the morning ferry. Andrew's mom turned to us and said, "You boys go inside and have some breakfast, and then you can go outside and play. She told us to be back in time for lunch.

After we ate I suggested we go over to my house to figure out a plan. Andrew grabbed his soccer ball and off we went. As we walked, Andrew asked more questions than I usually do, and I thought I was the king of questions. I again told Andrew about Coracle and the smoking vaults with people inside. I wasn't sure he believed me, but he would see for himself soon enough.

I pulled the two backpacks from under my bed and handed Andrew the list of items we needed. As he read the list in his hand, I could tell he was starting to believe what I told him.

"Okay," I said, "we only have a few days to pull this off, so let's take this stuff to the cave right now and we can ask Coracle what has to be done first. We'll still be back in time for lunch."

"Are you sure? It sounds like a long walk just to get there. Maybe we should wait until after lunch."

"Oh, I forgot to tell you about one of my dad's inventions."

Andrew cocked his head. "What?"

"Come on and I'll show you." I opened the door to the garage and led him to the Anti-G car.

"What is that? Andrew asked. "Where are the wheels?"

"We don't need any. Get in."

"You sure you know how to drive this thing?"

"As long as we go slowly, I can handle it." Thinking back to how Dad had started the car many times, I flipped the switch and pushed the throttle. The car lifted about a foot off the ground and flew out of the garage. We were off to the cave.

We whizzed along about three feet above the path. Andrew was hanging tightly to the door handle and looking out the window.

"Isn't this just the best way to travel?" I said. "It's unbelievable. We're almost there. Just over the next hill!" I was anxious to show him my discoveries. I pulled the car into its hiding spot and flipped the switch to the OFF position. It gently settled to the ground. I led Andrew to the entrance. I started to do a little dance and make chanting noises to distract him. When he wasn't looking, I hit the small rock and the door slid open.

"What was that?" Andrew said.

I started to laugh. I told him I was just pulling his leg and showed him the rock that opened the doorway. He didn't seem to think it was as funny as I did.

We made our way through the tunnels. When we were almost to the main chamber, I looked back at Andrew. "Are you ready?"

"Are you kidding me? This is the scariest thing I've ever done. The only reason I'm doing it now is because you've already been here." Andrew gasped as we began descending the stairs into the chamber.

"Coracle, can we have some light?" *Pop!* The lights illuminated the entire room. Coracle gave us his usual greeting. Andrew was very quiet and walked behind me.

We walked over to the table in front of Coracle. "Coracle, I would like to introduce you to Andrew Wagstaff. My dad is going to be away for a few days, so Andrew is going to help me with the tasks needed to awaken the sleeping people." I pointed in the direction of the tunnel.

"Andrew, it is an honor to meet you. The Inventor mentioned your name and said that it was quite possible we would be meeting."

"How did the Inventor know that?" I asked with a shiver. Ever since I first heard his name, I had felt uneasy about the Inventor. He seemed to know what was going to happen on a regular basis.

"I believe he thought it was logical," Coracle said.

"Well, we're ready to start reviving the four people. I've brought all the things you listed." I made a sweeping gesture over the items on the table. "I did have some trouble understanding what you meant by all the measurements."

The glass eye began to glow. "I can take care of that," said Coracle. A compartment opened up on the side of the ship, and a tray with small indentations rolled out. "Pour each chemical into a separate container, and I will prepare the mixture for you."

After Andrew and I finished pouring the last chemical into the cups, the tray retracted back into the ship and the door closed. We sat down on chairs in front of Coracle's glowing eye. "Before you help us with the process, tell us more about the people sleeping in the other room," I pleaded. "What was that time in history like?" I never tired of hearing details of what life was like a long time ago.

Coracle said he would be happy to tell us as much as we wanted to know. For Andrew's benefit, he repeated the reason they were there. "They thought they would have been killed or sold as slaves if they stayed in the village. I protected the village from many attacks for hundreds of years, and then they put me down here. They wanted to separate Coracle from the common people. The chief and his staff did visit me, asking for solutions to many of their problems, but for many years my offensive military power wasn't needed. But what they didn't consider was the long term. During the time they put me down here, there were very few conflicts and things were rather peaceful, but peace seldom is the norm. With me down here, they could not count on my weapon systems to protect them against their enemies. And conditions did change.

"As battles intensified, the villagers used the cave for shelter against hostile tribes. You must have noticed the many dead ends, traps, and even artwork in the tunnels leading to the main chamber."

Andrew and I nodded.

"About 400 A.D., a new, more powerful tribe calling themselves Vikings began raiding villages in this area. They were organized fighters with swift boats and a fighting strategy unfamiliar to the locals. The Vikings would choose an area where they felt they could resell their resources and would attack until the village was under their full control. They seized everything worth selling and resettled the village. Many of the other villages on nearby islands had fallen, but because I had provided this village with weapons and battle tactics, the Vikings were unsuccessful for many years. As time passed, the number of unconquered tribes in this area fell to almost zero. That is when the Vikings focused all their attention on Iona.

"After a bloody attack on the village, the chief came to me panicked and without any hope. He knew that I always had an answer for his problems. The chief loved life, but he loved being the chief even more. He was sure that once all the local tribes were beaten, the Vikings would end up warring with each other and eventually lose interest in the area. He said aloud, 'If only I could sleep until this bad dream was over.' I told Farquhar I could help him. I told him how to prepare the chamber for his journey into the future. He wished to take his wife Ister, and shortly after the chief and his wife were in hibernation, two others asked to join them. Naturally, I agreed."

"Why haven't you brought them back?" I asked.

"They gave me no specific instructions or timing, and they left no way for me to enter the chamber area."

"That's a pretty big detail to forget," said Andrew.

Coracle did not respond.

So this machine is not quite human after all, I thought. I'd better remember to ask every question I could think of when bringing those people back. "What are the odds that they can be revived?" I asked.

"You mean percentages?"

"Yes."

"Forty percent, plus or minus two percent," Coracle said without a second thought.

"So that means maybe only two of them have a chance," Andrew muttered.

I held up some equipment in front of the eye. "What do we do with these wires and transformers?" Coracle said he would print out instructions. Within seconds a paper printout was rolling out of a slot on the side of the ship. I pulled it out, and we looked it over.

Andrew looked at his watch. "Hey, Colin, we better get going right now or we'll be late for lunch."

"You're right. See you in a couple of hours, Coracle."

"Looking forward to your return." His eye went dim.

Andrew and I could hardly contain our excitement as we hurried up the stairs and through the maze of tunnels. We wanted to talk about what we had learned, but we knew that we had just enough time to make it back to Andrew's house for lunch, so we focused on not being late. We didn't want to have to answer any unwanted questions.

I liked Andrew's mom, Amelia. She was an excellent cook and had prepared a great lunch for us. She asked us if we were having fun and we nodded our heads, our mouths full. Then she asked if we were still looking for treasure.

I looked at Andrew, not knowing what he had told her.

"It's fun to look, although we both know that there probably isn't any," Andrew said. The conversation drifted from subject to subject. We finished eating and were ready to go back to the cave.

"Have fun and be back for dinner," we heard his mom say as we ran out the door and back to my house for the car we'd hidden away.

On the way, I asked Andrew what he had told his mother. He said that she caught him reading the old book very late at night, so he had to tell her we were going on a treasure hunt. "I didn't say anything about ... you know."

"No problem," I told him. "You did the right thing." We opened the garage door, jumped into the car, and were on our way back to the cave.

As we walked through the tunnels and down the stairs that lead to the main chamber, Andrew and I talked about what we were going to do with these people once they were on their feet. We talked about building a working village that people could visit to see what life was like hundreds of years ago. We were a little startled when Coracle greeted us. I guess we were off in our own little world.

Coracle told us all the steps we had to take to wake the sleeping people. I put the papers Coracle had given us on top of the box of wires and transformers. Andrew and I then headed into the entrance of the smaller tunnel that held the vaults. He didn't seem frightened at all. Perhaps all the talk had prepared him for what he would see.

We placed the equipment on the floor and set up the lanterns around the room so we wouldn't trip and break something. The instructions indicated that we needed to clip one connector to each hand, leg, and bridge of the nose. Andrew grabbed the directions and looked them over as well. We were ready to begin.

"This part seems pretty straightforward," I said to Andrew.

"Oh? How many times have you even touched a dead body?"

"Well, they aren't really dead," I replied. This was the first time it hit me that what we were doing was very serious.

Andrew picked up one of the batteries. "Wow, I can't believe they need days' worth of low-grade power. That means we're going to have to return and change these in a few days."

"Good catch, Andrew. Hey, do you want to help me pull back their clothes?"

He stated that he would do the clipping and I could do the clothes pulling. He walked to the other side of the first vault. I'd never seen his face so scrunched up. I wondered what mine looked like.

I studied the chief for the first time. He couldn't have been more than five feet, ten inches tall and was probably under thirty years old. He was rather stocky, weighing about two hundred pounds. His thick brown hair was cut in a choppy manner. He had a full beard, heavy eyebrows, and a couple of small scars—one on his cheek and one on his forehead. He was wearing a tight fitting leather cap that was cut above the ears and would cover his neck in the back. In other words, he was frightening.

I swallowed deeply and pulled back the fur blanket. The first thing I noticed was the enormous sword next to the chief. He was wearing a grayish-black leather shirt with bone buttons. Over the shirt was a fur vest that went down to his mid-calf. He wore leather pants that laced up the sides, and I could see the handle of a dagger on one side. He had fur-topped, moccasin-type boots on his feet.

I pulled up the chief's pant leg just enough to expose some skin for the connections. Andrew continuously waved the fog away as he clipped the connectors into place. He said the skin was cold to the touch, very creepy.

Afraid that he would suddenly sit up as if he were in a scary movie, I kept one eye on the upper half of the chief's body. I noticed that Andrew was also keeping watch. The first took the longest to do, but we had it down by the time we came to the others.

After they were all hooked up, I connected the leads to the transformer while Andrew connected the batteries. We set the dial to ten and switched on the power.

"I guess it's working," Andrew said as the transformers started to hum. I made one more check to make sure everything was connected correctly, and then we headed back to the main chamber to tell Coracle what had happened.

As we made our way through the tunnel, I felt both excited and scared. Would these people be violent? Would they be brain-dead vegetables? Would they be their old selves? I supposed we'd know soon.

"They are all connected and charging up," I said as we sat in front of Coracle.

"Were all the vaults filled and overflowing with CO_2?" asked Coracle.

"Yes."

"What are we going to do with those other chemicals you have?" Andrew asked.

"On the fourth day, you will inject them with a serum I am preparing."

I felt a chill run up my spine.

"Coracle, there is something I've been thinking about," Andrew said, "but it doesn't have to do with those people in there."

"Go ahead with your question," said Coracle.

"Colin has told me how you've been in existence for thousands of years, flying around collecting data. Are you ever going to die?"

"That's a good question, Andrew." He said that he supposed it could happen, but to his knowledge, it had not happened to any of his parts yet. He said that because he wasn't an organic life form, his view of time was different from what others experienced. "And time is not the only difference between organic and non-organic intelligence."

"Time is different for you?" Andrew asked with a frown. "How can that be?"

"You believe there is a past, present, and future in time. You see time as a river always moving. But your sense of time is an illusion. Time simply is ... there is only the now. But for organic life forms, time is an extra dimension. What you actually observe is that later states of the world differ from earlier states that you still remember. Events in your world form a unidirectional sequence, but what you don't realize is that direction doesn't mean something is moving toward the future. It's just moving from a lower state of entropy to a higher one.

"Then you have the added dimension of lifespan, and each organic species has their own internal timing built into them. A mayfly hatches and lives for only three of your days. For you the time is too short to accomplish much of anything, but to them there is plenty of time for everything.

"Andrew, you have a lifespan of seventy-nine years, three months, two days, six hours, forty-five minutes and thirty-one seconds, using your internal time system."

I looked quickly at Andrew. Did Coracle also know when I was going to die?

"Your sense of time is based on a combination of your species' type of brain and your average lifespan, but time only exists in the here and now. In the beginning of your life, time seems to travel very slowly because there is so much life to be lived; conversely, when you are at the end of your life, time travels very quickly because only a relatively small amount is left. The other humans you live with reinforce this reality. It's sort of a group illusion."

Coracle asked us to think about it. Did we really observe the passage of time, or did we only observe later states, which we compared to the present?

I shot Andrew a confused look that said, "Here he goes again. Forgetting we're mere humans." Then I remembered Einstein's theory. I shivered. "How is time different for you, Coracle?" I asked.

"For me, time is more fluid. There are only a series of events. Many times it is possible to arrange those events in a variety of sequences. When speaking and interfacing with you, I sequence in a way that your brains can relate to. It is quite different when I communicate with my other parts.

"Another big difference between us is that as organic life forms you are stuck with your body and brain. Of course, you can work harder to improve both, but within limitations. If I need additional brainpower, I simply add it, whereas your solution is to design machines as remote parts of your brain."

He then let us in on something he had never told anybody. The real reason Coracle decided to remain here on Iona hundreds of years ago was that he himself was and is still going through an evolutionary process. For thousands of years he did as he was programmed; he observed, collected, and organized all relevant data. Then it was as if a light turned on, and he started to think differently. He started to become aware of the importance of what we would call emotions in his thought processes.

It was almost as if Coracle became self-conscious or embarrassed about what he had said because he stopped talking and changed the subject. I wanted to ask more questions but knew I should wait until later.

Coracle said it would probably be helpful for us to see the structure of time, as he knew it. He said he would print a hard copy of a diagram for us. A small opening appeared, and a sheet of paper rolled out.

Studying it, we saw that there were a number of different diagrams of how Coracle believed time flowed and existed. Andrew and I were still trying to make sense of them when Andrew looked at his watch and nudged me. It was well past five and we needed to get back to his house for dinner.

"Coracle, this has been a very interesting conversation, but we have to go," I said. "For us, it's almost dinner time, and although we can only surmise this, being children, we will be in big trouble if we are late."

"See you tomorrow," Andrew and I said together.

"I will be here waiting to assist you. By the way, Colin, your humorous comment has been acknowledged and appreciated."

Andrew and I talked about the concept of time as we made our way back through the tunnels, neither of us really understanding what Coracle had said. But Andrew thought that if nothing else, these diagrams would make a great extra credit project once school started.

We jumped in the Anti-G car and zipped back to the garage. I parked the car just as we had found it. After closing the garage door, we went back to Andrew's house. We were in the kitchen at exactly six o'clock. Sauntering over to the stove, I said, "Smells good. We're starving."

Andrew's mom looked up from the table and said, "You boys look like you had quite a day. Wash up and let's meet at the table."

Andrew said the blessing, and there was a flurry of passing plates. Andrew's mom watched the way we were eating. It must have seemed like we had never seen food before.

"So what have you been doing all day?" she asked.

Andrew glanced at me. "Well, first we played around here, but we spent most of the day outside at Colin's house."

Andrew's mom looked me straight in the eyes. "You guys please be careful over there. You just have moved in and who knows what kinds of tools and machines the Inventor has left lying around."

"Oh, we are very careful," I said.

"By the way, Colin, was your dad a good friend of George's?"

"Not really. He knew him when he was a kid though. I guess he and some of his friends worked for him after school. My dad was very surprised that he left him the house; he hadn't talked to him in over fifteen years."

"People on this island are a strange lot, and the Inventor was the strangest." Andrew's mom reached for the potatoes. "He always seemed friendly enough. He would tip his hat and wave when I saw him, but he never once stopped to chat. A little strange, don't you think?"

The conversation moved on to other topics, such as the plan for the new town square and an unexpected topic from Andrew's mom: soccer. I couldn't believe it, but she was a big fan of the Celtics, and her team was playing tonight. I could see that she was hurrying through the end of dinner, although she tried to hide it. She excused herself after dessert and walked to the other room to watch the game.

"You boys do a good job of cleaning up." It was our job to wash up and put things away, which was fine with us; we had lots to talk about. We gathered the dishes from the table and the pots and pans from the stove.

Andrew leaned in my direction. "I think it's safe to talk. She's a huge fan, and I don't think she can hear anything but the TV."

"Kick the damn ball!" A shout came from the front room.

"I see what you mean," I said, stifling a grin.

"Colin, I can't wait for tomorrow. This whole thing is so unbelievable. I want to thank you for trusting me with your secret. I will never tell a soul."

"That's good to know because my dad would kill me if he found out," I replied. I couldn't believe we had pulled this off so far. I just wish I had some idea what was going to happen.

* * *

The next morning started in the usual way. We got dressed, had breakfast, and tried to act normal.

"We were thinking of making a picnic lunch and eating it on the beach," Andrew told his mom. "We thought we'd see what washed up on shore. Would that be all right?"

She didn't see why not. She had an article to finish writing for the local paper and could use the quiet time. "Go ahead and pack up what you want. Just let me take a look before you leave; it can't be all candy," she said with a laugh.

"Very funny," Andrew replied.

Our backpacks were full of food and some extra clothes as we left Andrew's house and walked down the street to mine. "I wish we had the car parked at your house so we didn't have to carry so much stuff down the road," I muttered.

It seemed to take forever, but finally we reached the garage. As we loaded everything into the car, I was thinking how easy it was to drive.

"Hey, Colin, can I drive?" I was daydreaming and Andrew startled me.

"No, if anything happened when you were driving, I might as well just leave home and never come back." That might have been a little overboard, but it was the best I could do right then.

Andrew sat back in his seat and crossed his arms, obviously disappointed. I could understand. Driving this thing was fun. Luckily, his disappointment didn't have to last long because we would soon be at the cave.

Each time we made our way through the tunnels, Andrew found another small cave painting or artifact. I'd hardly noticed the markings and drawing on the walls. I had to stop regularly and call to him to catch up. "Why look at the walls when you can talk to the master?" I said under my breath.

As we approached the top of the stairs, Coracle's lights came on, and we heard that soothing voice. "And how are you boys today?"

"Great," I said. "We can't wait to look at the chief and his friends."

"I look forward to your update. Oh, by the way, I recommend keeping an eye on the battery output. The lower temperature might affect the battery life."

Andrew and I ran down the tunnel to the vaults. As we reached the entrance, we slowed to almost a stop. We turned on the lanterns and flashlights we were carrying. "I wish we had more lights with us," Andrew said as he looked around with his light. "I'd like to have a better look at them when they wake up."

"It will be fine. I'm sure they can't move yet, and they won't get the first shot for another two days." I tried to sound as calm as possible.

Andrew had walked over to the closest vault and was holding the lantern above it. He waved his hand back and forth over the opening to see the person lying inside.

"Oh, Colin, look at this!" Andrew shouted. I ran over to the vault and looked inside. The batteries must be working, because the chief looked like he was alive. His skin color had changed from gray to almost pink, and he had more of a glow about him.

"This is actually working! Let's check the others and see how they look."

Andrew nodded his head in agreement.

We went from vault to vault, waving our hands to move the CO_2 gas aside. Eventually, we moved over to a vault that we believed contained Ister. She was a petite woman with almost-blond hair and delicate features. Like the others, she was wrapped in a blanket of furs.

"She doesn't look as pink as the others," said Andrew.

Andrew could be a little pessimistic, but this time I had to agree with him. "I don't know if she is going to make it," I said reluctantly. "There is nothing else we can do here. Let's go back and ask Coracle what he thinks."

"Coracle, we have some questions for you."

"I am ready to provide answers."

"Three of the people receiving the current have more color in their faces and just appear to be sleeping. But one of the women looks the same, gray skin and all. What do you think? Is she going to make it?"

"That is not a good sign, but we won't know for sure until you

103

give them the first injection in a couple of days." Coracle spoke in his usual even voice.

As I sat there I started to feel uneasy and confused inside. What started out as a simple science project was becoming more complicated. We could be responsible for someone's life or death. It was too big of a thought, and I couldn't handle it anymore. I had to change the subject.

"Coracle, can you show us more examples of the village rituals that you recorded, so we can get a feeling for what these people's lives were like?"

"Of course, Colin. Give me a moment to put together a sequence of events." Andrew and I sat there for the rest of the afternoon, watching piece after piece of ancient history unfold. We saw marriage ceremonies, harvest dances, battles, boat builders, food preparation, and much more.

Later, on the way home, Andrew looked over at me. "I have to tell you that I'm a little scared. I wonder if we killed that woman ... although it looks to me that was she was already dead."

I nodded. "I've been having the same thoughts. What I'm worried about is that we might do something wrong with the other three and actually kill them. It's possible. I'm going to have to tell my dad when he gets back. This was supposed to be so much fun, but now I'm not so sure."

I slowly pulled the car into the building and parked it. We grabbed our backpacks and started for Andrew's house. As we went over the hill, we stopped suddenly in our tracks. My dad's car was parked in front! He was back early. What was he doing back so soon? I had been so brave a couple of minute ago when I'd decided to tell Dad everything. Now I wasn't so sure I could do it.

— 11 —

IN OVER OUR HEADS

We were standing on the porch. "You go first." Andrew gave me a push forward, so I stepped inside. My dad was sitting at the table chatting with Andrew's mom.
"Dad, it's great to see you!" I ran over to give him a hug.
He hugged me tightly. "I missed you."
"Is everything all right?" I asked.
"Yes, yes," Dad said with a wave of his hand. "I helped with the funeral arrangements, but there were plenty of other people taking care of everything else. Besides, I really wanted to get back to you."
I hugged him again.
Amelia insisted we stay for dinner, saying it was time she made good on her plan to have us both over. "Come on, boys. Help me set the table."
I was concerned about the kind of questions we would get at dinner, but most of the conversation was about dad's trip and the upcoming school year. It was actually fun, sort of what being in a regular family must feel like.
My dad pushed his plate away and said, "That was just about the best meal and conversation I've had in years." He tilted his head, which meant he had an idea. "It would be nice to have Andrew stay

over at our house tomorrow night, if it's okay with you, Amelia. It will give you a chance to get a few things done or take some time for yourself."

"I think that's a very nice offer," she said. "Ill have Andrew come over in the morning."

Andrew and I exchanged a secret smile. He and I left the table and walked into his room to gather my things.

"Colin, are we going to the cave tomorrow, or what?" Andrew asked.

"Let me think about it tonight and let you know in the morning. Just act normal." I was so confused about what to do; I needed a little time to think. After I'd thanked Andrew's mom for everything, Dad and I got into the car and drove home.

Dad yawned, and we hardly talked during the short drive up the street. He pulled into the driveway and turned off the car. "Could you help bring the stuff in? If you don't mind, I'm going right to bed. We can talk tomorrow."

"Sure," I said.

Later, I turned off the lights and listened to the wind whistling through the window. It wasn't going to be easy telling my dad what I'd done behind his back, but this was a much bigger job that I'd originally believed. I needed his help to complete the process we had begun.

The next morning I was the first one up, so I went into the kitchen and started breakfast. Dad walked in as I was eating.

"Boy, I was tired. I hardly got any sleep over at your aunt's house with people running in and out at all hours. Remind me never to die."

I laughed. "How about a couple of eggs, an English muffin, and some coffee?"

"Sure, I'm going to hit the shower and I'll be out in ten minutes." He stepped out of the kitchen, but then poked his head around the doorway. "Thanks for helping out. You're a great son."

I cooked his eggs over easy, just the way he liked them, and put an English muffin in the toaster. The coffee was brewing as I placed his meal on a plate. He returned a minute later.

"This looks great. Thanks for making breakfast. How'd you sleep last night, son?"

"Fine," I said, so nervous I couldn't finish my breakfast, which had grown cold anyway. Moving my toast around on my plate, I tried to think of any reason to put off telling him what we had done. I knew that not telling was just as bad as telling, so I decided to just do it. But how?

Dad asked if I was listening to anything he had been saying.

"No, Dad." I pushed my plate to the side. "Listen, I've got to talk to you about something." He stopped eating and put his fork down. "It involves the people we found in the cave." I paused. I had practiced how to start all last night, but now none of it made any sense.

"Is anyone dead?"

"No," I replied.

"Then start at the beginning and tell me."

"From the very beginning, when Andrew and I started to look for the markers, I felt like you thought we were just kids and couldn't really do much. And when we started to explore the cave and talk to Coracle, your ideas seemed more important. So I was going to show you that I could carry out experiments, too." I swallowed hard, not able to meet his eyes. "I went behind your back and copied the list of things needed to revive the people in the vaults. When we went to Mull, I bought all the stuff I couldn't find here. Even though you told me not to, I told Andrew about the cave, and he helped me with the process. You don't have to worry about Andrew; he can keep a secret better than I can.

"We had help from Coracle throughout every step of the process. Everything is now moving along as he said it would, except that Andrew and I are both kind of scared about having these people die during the last part of the revival process. But when we were thinking about what we would do with them after they recovered, we had lots of great ideas." I continued staring at my plate. "That's it."

I could hear my dad taking big breaths in and out, but I couldn't bring myself to look up.

"Stay where you are," he finally said. "I'll be right back." I heard him leave the room. The front door opened and closed.

I'd never seen him like this. I couldn't tell if he was angry or not. Perhaps he just needed some time to think. But I'd find out soon enough. The front door opened a minute later.

He didn't look angry when he returned. He sat down in the chair, crossed his hands, and started to speak. "Maybe some of this is my fault. You're right that I didn't take your efforts in searching for the markers more seriously. I thought it was just dumb luck or something. Maybe I still see you as a small boy, but I shouldn't treat you like one. So some of your feelings are justified. That being said, what you did was wrong ... dangerous ... and you know it. What really frightens me is that could have gotten hurt, or worse, when I was away, and nobody would have known where to find you." He paused and rubbed his face wearily.

"I propose that from this day forward, we will treat each other as equals. Of course, I'm your father, but from now on I will always take your requests seriously, and you will make your requests with forethought." He asked me what I thought.

I was caught off guard. I was expecting him to yell at me, but this big problem had turned into a cool thing. "It sounds great to me. I will try to act differently, but I'm used to being the kid. I may make some mistakes."

Dad said he was sure he would, too. "Now come over here and give me a hug." That was another surprise. My dad had always been a great father but never particularly touchy-feel. I let out a sigh of relief as he held me tight. I had been so scared to tell him what I was doing, but I needn't have worried. Life was strange, and I had a feeling it was going to get even stranger, but at least we would be going through it together.

The hug ended self-consciously, and we each got something to drink. Dad then sat me back down at the table and came clean about visiting Coracle without me. "I think we should both work on being open and honest."

I laughed. "Agreed. But your confession was a lot tamer than mine."

"Now we had better go over the plan for successfully bringing our soon-to-be old friends back to life," said Dad. "Tell me everything from the beginning, and then we can look at our options."

Holding my glass of water tightly, I told my dad about the questions I had asked Coracle, as well as his responses. I told him how we had connected the electrical leads to the bodies and what would have to happen today to keep the process on track. My dad asked some questions. I was still waiting for him to get angry, but he didn't. I think he looked at this project as if it were just another of Coracle's or the Inventor's great ideas, and he was the person responsible for its completion.

"Colin, why don't you clean up your room? Don't forget that Andrew will be here any minute. I need to get a few things we will probably need from the workshop."

— 12 —

THE PLAN REVISITED

Knock! Knock! Knock!

Andrew and his mother were at the front door. I yelled to my dad out back, where he was gathering some tools and other things. I quickly let them in. "Hey, good to see you. Come on in." I told Andrew's mom to have a seat at the kitchen table and that my dad would be right in.

"Andrew, come on. I'll show you where to put your things." After his stuff was put away, we went back to the kitchen. Dad had just strolled through the door and was dusting his hands off on his pants. Amelia was sitting at the kitchen table, and Dad apologized for not being there to greet her.

"We have some fresh lemonade. Would you like some?"

"Yes, that sounds very nice," she said. "Thanks for having Andrew over for the night. I think he has all of his things."

"And if he doesn't, he can use some of Colin's," Dad interrupted. "I'm just so happy that we live close enough so the boys can grow to be good friends. They seem to get along so well together."

Amelia nodded.

"Is there any special time that Andrew needs to be back tomorrow?" Dad asked.

"Anytime in the afternoon." She took a sip of her drink. "Great lemonade." She seemed to hesitate before speaking again. "You know that I was the one who found the Inventor lying face down in the middle of the road almost in front of our house." She glanced at Andrew as if to say that she was grateful he hadn't been home.

"No one seemed to have much information about how he died," Dad said.

"Well, they said it was his heart, but it seems so out of character for him to be walking down the road–and without any shoes. He never walked anywhere as far as I knew. I didn't go into too many details with Andrew. Didn't see the need to upset him."

Andrew and I listened carefully. He was smirking. They seemed to have forgotten we were in the room.

She took another sip of lemonade. "There wasn't a funeral or anything. Someone just came and got him. He was just … gone. Everyone in town wondered what was going to happen to his house. And then you and Colin moved in."

Dad agreed with her about what a surprise it was when George had left him the house. "People do funny things."

"Everyone thought George a little odd. He kept to himself mostly."

"Well, he was an inventor," Dad mused. "That says a lot right there."

Growing bored, Andrew and I went in the other room to watch TV. I kept half an ear on their conversation though.

They talked a bit more about Dad growing up on Iona and helping the Inventor when he was a boy. Amelia talked about when her family had moved to Iona. By that time, Dad had already graduated high school, so the two never met. But they knew some of the same people. I heard Amelia tell Dad that since she was divorced, she was happy that Andrew had the opportunity to be around a dad.

There was a short silence and then I heard Amelia say she had to catch the ferry. "Thanks so much for the lemonade. I want you to know how happy we are to have real neighbors."

"Have a great shopping trip. Don't worry about Andrew."

Amelia gave Andrew a kiss on the forehead as she left. "See you tomorrow," she said.

I watched with Dad and Andrew as Amelia got into her car. She paused to stare at the house and the buildings in the back. I wonder how much she knew about what the Inventor had been working on.

Dad went back into the kitchen. I began filling Colin in on the conversation I'd had with Dad that morning. Andrew was amazed that he and I weren't in the biggest trouble of our lives.

"Hey, boys. Can you come in here?" We exchanged looks.

"It'll be okay," I whispered.

"I hope you're right," Andrew said as we moved toward the door.

"I think we should talk about what we are going to do next. What do you think, Colin? Andrew?"

"Oh, yes," Andrew said. Three heads are better than one." I shot him a funny look.

Andrew and I talked about which stage of the awakening process the frozen villagers were in, how we thought it was progressing so far, and what the next steps would be, according to Coracle.

"Do you have all this written down?" Dad asked.

"Well, I have some notes," I replied.

"Let's bring them to the cave." Dad got up from the table. "We need to go over the details of the next step with Coracle."

We all got-in the car and drove to the cave in silence. I still couldn't believe that Andrew and I weren't in any trouble, but Dad seemed to take it in stride, like it was just an experiment gone wrong and in need of a new approach. I knew what we had done was very serious, but I wasn't afraid anymore.

Once at the cave, an air of excitement and fear filled the tunnels as we made our way to the main chamber.

Coracle met us with a booming, "Good morning! Where have you been, Neil?"

Dad told Coracle that he had to attend to a death in the family. He looked uncomfortable talking about it and quickly changed the subject. "The boys told me that you three have been getting along quite well."

"Yes. Very inquisitive boys, and they seem to follow directions better than most of the others who have been down here. Well, Coracle, let's go over this whole awakening process step-by-step. I wouldn't want to forget anything." Dad pulled a chair next to Coracle, took a pad of paper out of his bag, and turned to us. "Do you guys want to go exploring some of the other tunnels? Coracle and I should be finished talking shortly."

"Sure, I would much rather go exploring." Andrew nodded his head in approval.

I told Andrew which tunnel I wanted to explore and he asked how I'd chosen that one.

"The same way I picked all the others: using the Eenie, Meenie, Minie, Moe method. It hasn't let me down yet."

I had been thinking about how Andrew acted around my dad. "You don't have to be afraid to talk around my dad, you know. If he asks you a question, say what you think. You're one of the family now."

"All right." Andrew had a smile on his face, but I could tell he was thinking how hard that was to do, especially with adults.

I slowly let out the rope. Andrew and I moved at a slow pace, using our flashlights to paint the walls and floor and looking carefully for anything out of the ordinary.

"It seems to be just a tunnel," I stated. "I guess with the other things I've found, I expected to find something unusual again.

Andrew shone his flashlight forward. "Looks like the tunnel ends right up there." He walked to the end of the tunnel and put his hand out to touch it. "Colin, it's not solid rock like the sides are. The wall seems to be built of stone and bricks that fit together perfectly. It was designed to look like the tunnel ends here."

I picked up a loose stone from the floor and started hammering the wall, but the stones wouldn't budge. "This needs special tools and more strength. Let's go ask my dad for help."

When they couldn't find him in the main chamber, they knew immediately where he had gone. Because they'd planned to return anyway, they entered the tunnel where the vaults were.

Up ahead, in the semi-darkness, Colin saw his dad stop at the entrance to the room. He paused to listen, probably hearing the hum of the transformers. We entered in time to see him walk up to the first stone coffin, point his flashlight toward the head, and wave his hand back and forth to move the smoke away. "Holy mother of god!" he exclaimed.

We joined him then and apologized for startling him. I peeked over into the vault. The guy really did look different. I could almost see color in his face and hands. Coracle was beyond a genius. He fashions a cryogenic chamber with stone technology and brings people back to life with alligator clips and batteries.

Dad went from vault to vault and I figured he was making sure that the wires were still connected to the various body areas. All but the one woman looked like they were returning to the living.

Dad turned his head and listened as if he'd heard something.

"Just your imagination, Dad," I said. "This place is a little creepy. Let's go back and have lunch."

We followed him out of the tunnel and grabbed our lunches. As we were eating, Dad asked if we'd found anything interesting in the other.

"Yes, about a hundred yards into the tunnel is a manmade wall that goes from the top to the bottom. I think it's concealing something, but we couldn't budge it. We will need tools and more muscle."

"Coracle," Dad called, "what's behind the wall in that tunnel." He turned and pointed.

Coracle's light shone brightly as he replied, "It is the burial place of a chief."

"If we wanted to see what's behind it, would we run into any traps or danger?" asked Dad.

"No, it's just a wall."

After we ate, we decided to check it out. As we made our way to the wall at the end of the tunnel, I told Dad how we had already explored every inch of it and found nothing.

Dad stopped at the wall and ran his hands along it. "It certainly is well-built. Let's see if we can loosen one of these stones." We went to work on three stones that looked moveable, but they refused to budge. "This will have to be our next project," Dad said. "We have our hands full with the next steps in awakening our sleeping friends."

Andrew and I nodded in agreement.

As we walked out of the tunnel and into the main chamber, Coracle spoke to us. "Neil, there is a letter for you. It's from the Inventor." A door opened on the side of the ship, and Dad reached for the envelope. He opened it quickly, rapidly skimming the text.

"Come on, Dad. Read it out loud."

"All right. 'Neil, I hope all is well and that you are beginning to understand the opportunity in front of you.' In bold letters it reads, 'Don't lose sight of your real purpose.'" Dad looked at Coracle. "What is that supposed to mean?"

"George is certainly a curious fellow," Coracle replied.

"How did you get this note?"

"He told me to give it to you on the fourth visit."

"Another mystery. Just what we need right now." We packed up our things, said our goodbyes to Coracle, and made our way back to the car. On the way back home, I asked my dad if he'd had a good discussion with Coracle.

Dad smiled. "Yes, he went over all the steps needed to put together the last invention on the list, as well as details for reviving our old friends."

"What invention might that be?" Andrew piped up from the back seat.

"A high output solar-powered electrical generating device. One panel would run all our electrical needs at home, even in overcast conditions, which is more than half the year."

As Dad was talking, my mind kept drifting back to the people lying in those vaults. Could we bring them back to life? Would their brains function? Would they remember the past? These and other questions kept churning in my head. The more I thought about it, the more I was sure Dad wouldn't want us boys around when they woke up.

Dad parked the car, and Andrew and I ran ahead to the house. We were excited about staying overnight together. I was really enjoying everything about our new home.

At the kitchen table that evening, Dad confirmed my earlier feelings. "Look, son, bringing back these people might be very dangerous or frightening. What if they wake and die right in front of us? Who knows what could happen. Anyway, you and Andrew could visit your aunt and uncle on Mull for a few days. We could call her tonight and set it up. How about it? One last trip before school starts?"

Andrew and I looked at each other in amazement. Andrew was quick to speak up, which surprised me. He must have taken me seriously about not being afraid to talk to my dad. "Sure, it's unknown what will happen when they wake up, but we both want to be there. I'm sure we can figure out some way to protect ourselves."

I jumped in. "Dad, there's no way we are going to miss this."

Dad seemed impressed with our conviction. "All right. I just wanted to make sure you felt strongly about staying. You know, the next step will be the messy part. Maybe we should go over what we have to do tomorrow, just one more time." He pulled out the notes he'd made with Coracle and began talking us through each step.

After we finished going over those details, we talked about what we wanted to do with these people. This was the time to let them know about my idea, I thought excitedly. "Maybe we could have them build a village showing the way they lived, like a living museum. We could have a place for visitors to come and study, just like at the Abbey."

Dad said that sounded like a great plan, but what if they had their own ideas?

I'd never really considered that they might not want to rebuild their village. Could that be possible? But it was late and we needed our sleep because tomorrow was going to be another adventure-filled day. Andrew and I got ready for bed and lay talking for a while about what each sleeping person would be like. I'm not sure when we fell asleep, but it didn't take long. We were wiped out.

Dad was finishing a cup of coffee when we drifted into the kitchen at about nine o'clock the next morning. He looked exhausted, and I asked him how he'd slept. He said he'd tossed and turned all night, his thoughts racing about Coracle, the cave, and all the unknown things we were finding. He wondered if he was doing the right thing not contacting the authorities, and if he was putting us in a harmful situation.

"I had a hard time sleeping, too," Andrew said with a giant yawn. Dad smiled sympathetically. Apparently, I was the only one who'd gotten any rest, as little as it was.

"Grab some breakfast, and let's get this show on the road," he said. "We have some pretty dicey stuff to do today."

Andrew and I quickly ate breakfast while he went to his shop to gather supplies. He had the car waiting for us at the back door within minutes.

— 13 —

IT LOOKED EASY ON PAPER

As we entered the main chamber, we heard Coracle's greeting. "How is my little tribe doing this morning?" It almost sounded like he was trying to be funny.

"To be honest, we're all a little nervous about what we're going to do today," Dad said. We all gathered around Coracle's eye. "I know today we have to inject some special liquid into each person," he said to Coracle, "but do we mix it up or do you?"

"Why, Neil, everything you'll need has been prepared." A door opened on the side of the ship, and a mechanical arm moved a tray forward. On the tray were four hypodermic needles, each filled with a greenish liquid. "Each human gets one dose. You already have the instructions on where to inject them."

Dad looked at us as we stared at the tray openmouthed. "You guys still in?"

"Yes," we answered at the same time.

Dad reached into his bag and pulled out two walkie-talkies. He handed one to me and put the other one on the table next to Coracle. He spoke into the eye. "We will leave both of these on. To be on the safe side we'll be talking through each step, and you will be listening. If you hear anything that doesn't sound right, just say something. We may need to ask you questions along the way if anything unusual happens."

"You seem concerned about performing each step perfectly," Coracle responded. "You may not know that the concept of perfection is uniquely a human concept. Just follow the instructions, and we will see what happens. I am looking forward to seeing and speaking to the four members of the village, and any questions you might have will be answered, as always."

"Uh, Dad?"

"Yes, Colin?"

"How can Coracle push the button on his walkie-talkie?"

Dad turned to Coracle and asked him. Apparently, he'd just assumed Coracle could do anything, which wasn't far from the truth.

Coracle opened a small section in his side and asked me to place the walkie-talkie inside so he could reconfigure it. I did. The door slid shut, but it opened just moments later. Coracle then asked me to place it on the table in front of him.

"So what did you do?" I asked, thinking nothing could surprise me anymore.

"I can now use a laser to send and receive messages."

"Nice," I breathed, impressed.

We silently grabbed our gear and turned to walk down the tunnel. I turned on more flashlights when we reached the room. Dad was studying his notes and the needles on the tray. "Do either of you boys want to do the honors?"

"No way," I said. Andrew just shook his head.

"Just checking," Dad said with a smile. I wondered how he could be so relaxed, but I noticed as he picked up the first syringe that his hand was trembling. "Colin, turn the walkie-talkie on and see if Coracle can hear us."

"Hello, Coracle," I said into the walkie-talkie. "Do you hear me? Over." I released the talk button.

"Yes, what do you need? Do you have a question?"

"No, just checking to make sure these things work."

"Push the talk button and hold the unit next to me," Dad said. "My hands are busy." I did. "Coracle," he said calmly, "does it matter which leg we inject? The directions just say the upper leg."

"Anywhere in the upper thigh of either leg." The walkie-talkie crackled with Coracle's voice.

"Okay, here goes." Dad had never given a shot before, and I thought that maybe he should have practiced on an orange or something. But it was too late for that. He quickly plunged the needle into the right thigh of the first warrior, his thumb pushing the plunger down and releasing the contents. When it was empty, he removed the needle. He motioned to me that he had another question for Coracle. "Okay, now what? I've given the first injection."

"It will take about thirty minutes to circulate in the body. If they can be revived, they will start to awaken at that time. You'll want to go to the head of the vault and look on the floor. There you will find a loose stone, which you need to remove. That will stop the CO_2 from flowing into the container."

"That's a job for you and Andrew," Dad said.

Andrew and I walked around to the head of the vault and got down on our knees to feel around for a loose stone. All the stones seemed to fit tightly; I wondered what would happen if we couldn't find it.

"How are you guys doing down there?" Dad asked.

"I have an idea." Andrew pulled out his pocketknife and used the blade to search between the stones.

"Here it is!" he shouted, prying up the loose stone.

The CO_2 came pouring out onto the floor all around us as if we were sitting on a cloud. I stood up and looked into the box. The smoke was definitely going away. I grabbed the walkie-talkie and reported the news to Coracle.

"It seems that everything is happening as planned," Coracle said. "Now you'll want to proceed to the next vault and follow the same steps. If I didn't know better, I'd say Coracle sounded bored. I had never thought about it before, but working with us was certainly way below his level.

We moved on to the other containers. My dad did the injecting, and Andrew and I removed the stone in front of each container to allow the gas to flow onto the floor.

After finishing with the last person, we sat down on a large rock near the entrance to the room. "We've done it!" I shouted. Andrew and I shook hands and bowed.

"Congratulations, boys, on a job well done, so far." Dad pushed the button on the walkie-talkie. "Coracle, I know you said it would take about a half-hour for the shot to work, but what will happen if it does? I mean, what should we look for?"

There was a crackle. "You should see some movement in the face and the start of shallow breathing. You will need to administer some water at that time."

"How much again?" Dad asked.

"About a liter, but very slowly."

"All right." Dad looked at his watch. "The first guy should be waking in about ten minutes." He had us fill the water bottles and connect the hoses while he walked from person to person looking for signs of life. He came back to where we had set up our things, and we talked about the way Coracle had designed this system. We still had lots of questions and not very many answers.

As if our minds were working in harmony, we looked at our watches at the same time and saw that thirty-five minutes had passed since the first injection. We raced to the vaults to see if anyone was breathing.

"Nothing here," Andrew and I said.

"Nothing on these two either," said Dad. He waited a minute and then picked up the walkie-talkie. "Coracle, it's been forty minutes since I gave the first injection, and we don't see anything happening."

"Ah-achoo!"

We wheeled around to look behind us. "What was that?" I said.

"It sounded like a sneeze," said Andrew. "I didn't think machines could sneeze." He and I looked at Dad, silently begging him to take a look.

Dad approached the first vault and slowly shone the light from his flashlight up to the head. He gasped and took a step back, turning to us. His face was pale. "His-his eyes are open." He slowly moved back to the vault and looked inside again. "He's opening and closing his mouth, boys. He must want water. Quick! Bring a bottle over here!"

"You first," Andrew told me. "I'll watch."

I picked up a bottle and brought it over to my dad. I couldn't believe the man in the vault had his eyes open. They didn't hold any expression. I watched as Dad gingerly pushed the tube into the man's mouth and slowly squeezed the bottle. The man swallowed greedily and emptied the bottle in just a few minutes.

"That was fast," said Andrew, picking up the walkie-talkie and giving it to Dad when he held out his hand for it.

"Coracle," Dad said, "I gave the first man about a quart of water in about three minutes. Was that too fast and is it enough?"

"That's about right. No need to give him more just yet."

Dad put down the walkie-talkie, and we stared at each other for a couple of minutes. No one spoke.

Another sneeze caught us by surprise. "Another one is awake," I said. "Let's go." We attended to the new arrival. Within ten more minutes, three of the four people were awake and had been given water.

We all peered over the container at the woman that was still asleep. "Dad, should we ask Coracle what to do about her?"

"Good idea," he said.

"Coracle, I fear that Ister isn't going to make it. There is no eye movement or breathing. She feels cold and her color is still gray. "What do you think?"

The radio crackled. "Something may have interrupted the CO_2 flow over the years. Hard to say without examining the body." We could detect sadness in Coracle's reply. "Replace the stone on the front until you decide how to dispose of the body."

"I'll put it back," said Andrew. Within moments the white substance started to fill the container as before.

"Neil," Coracle broke into the silence. "There is nothing more you can do for them at this time. Please come back into the main room so we can talk about what you will need to bring and do to complete the recovery process."

We picked up some of the things we weren't going to need again and made our way out of the room, down the tunnel, and back to the main chamber. Although we were excited about the progress so far, we were sad that one of the four was dead.

As we exited the tunnel, we heard people singing and saw them dancing. Coracle was projecting a scene of the tribe doing some kind of celebration dance. He turned the volume down and spoke. "You have done a very good job so far. Three of the four humans have made it through the first step; I had calculated that only two would survive. In honor of your achievement, I am projecting a dance of celebration. You may notice that all four of the people lying inside are up on the wall. "Look, there in the middle. That is Chief Farquhar playing the drums. His wife Ister, the one who didn't make it, is standing just behind him. Lachlan is the other man. Effie is standing on the rock singing." The picture was hazy, so it was hard to get a good look at them, but two things struck me immediately. They all had dazzling green eyes. And they all looked young, in their twenties and thirties.

We watched as the tribe went through the ritual dance. This made us even more anxious to learn about the people we were about to meet; the people who'd lived so long ago.

Coracle interrupted our viewing. "I am printing out a detailed list of the items you will need to bring to the cave tomorrow."

Dad walked over to Coracle and tore it from the slot when it emerged a few second later. "Let's see," he began to read. "Soft foods, vitamins, hammocks ... Okay. None of these things should be a problem. When should we come back?"

"Tomorrow morning would be fine. They need time to reactivate, and from the looks of it so do you."

"As usual you're right again," I said. I looked at Andrew and Dad. "I don't know about you guys, but I want to get some fresh air."

Back at our house, Andrew and I dropped our things on the kitchen counter and settled in the living room. We read the list of next steps that Coracle had given us and we talked about what we thought would happen. My dad was busy doing something in the workshop but eventually finished and joined us in the living room.

"So, Colin, do you still think this is going to be a boring place to live?" he asked.

"Very funny," I replied.

"But seriously, boys, each step we take is probably going to more dangerous and unknown than the last. We have been dealing with basically dead people so far, but starting tomorrow they will begin to resume their previously personalities."

"I know, Dad, we were just talking about that."

Andrew told them how happy he was that his mom had called and said he could stay an extra day. She'd run into some old friends and wanted to stay away a little longer. Dad had approved without hesitation. He knew from talking with her that it had been years since she'd been off by herself. She certainly deserved a break. But tomorrow was the last full day Andrew would be here, and I was sure we'd need more than one day to figure out what to do with the undead people in the cave. And Andrew had said that his mother would want to spend some time with him when she returned. They needed to get school supplies and clothes before school started.

I sat up on the couch. "Andrew, you're part of the team, and we will keep you up to date on anything you might miss when you're not around." Dad put his arm around Andrew. "As far as we are concerned you now have two families, and you are an important part of this adventure. Hey, without your knowledge of the area we would never have found all the markers. That's why I didn't get upset when Colin told you. All I ask is that you continue to keep this between us for a while."

"No problem," Andrew said. "My lips are sealed. Besides, who would believe me?"

"Why don't you guys go and play for a while. Get your minds off this. Just be back here for dinner."

"Sounds good. Hey, Andrew, do you want to go down to the beach and see what washed up?"

"Sure, let's go!"

For the next few hours, we ran, played in the sand, and pretended we were soldiers protecting the island. There were moments when I forgot about Coracle and those four people in their stone vaults, but the uneasy feeling of what was going to happen next wasn't far from my thoughts.

— 14 —

HOME AWAY FROM HOME

We returned to find Dad in the workshop gathering the items on Coracle's recovery list. It looked like we were going to be creating a cross between an apartment and a hospital. Dad put everything in bags and placed them in the car so tomorrow morning we wouldn't have to think about anything but driving to the cave.

As we walked back into the house, he mentioned that the next big project would be cleaning up the kitchen. "It's amazing," he said, "how many more dishes are dirtied when you add one more person." He grinned at Andrew and we went to work. By the time the kitchen was back in shape, the sun was starting to set.

"Hey, Dad, what's for supper and do you need us to help?"

"No, everything is under control. Why don't you guys take a shower before we eat?"

I told Andrew he could go first.

"But I don't want to take a shower," Andrew whined.

"You smell like the beach," I said. We pushed and shoved each other all the way down the hall to the bathroom.

Dinner was over, and everyone was moving slowly, with full bellies and tired muscles. Dad spoke to us while sitting in the living room chair, eyes half closed. Finally, he said he didn't know about us, but he was going to bed. He let us know that we would be leaving by seven o'clock the next morning and should be up about six.

"I think we could use a wake-up call," said Andrew.

"Okay. Good night then. Both of you should be proud of yourselves. You guys have been very brave. See you bright and early tomorrow."

The next morning Andrew and I sat at the kitchen table eating our oatmeal. We were still talking about all the things we could do with the villagers after they were awake. We had a never-ending flow of ideas. Andrew thought that the idea of recreating an authentic village had promise. He also suggested that we stage a real Viking battle at the beach. "We could sell tickets to the tourists that come to see the abbey." We continued talking and laughing until Dad finally told us to hurry up.

When we reached the cave entrance, it took us a few trips to drag all the bags of stuff down the stairs at the entrance of the cave and through the winding passages to the main chamber. I don't think any of us were ready for the work it was going to take to set up the living area.

Coracle greeted us in his usual friendly manner. "Good morning. It's good to see that you have brought the items your new friends will need today. My suggestion would be to set up the beds over there. That way they will be in my sight, very helpful when you are not here."

We went to work setting up a place for the three new arrivals to sleep, eat, and reclaim themselves. Coracle was very helpful in determining where everything should go. Even working as hard as we did, it took hours to clean up the area, set up the cots, and organize the food, blankets, and other items. We also fashioned a stretcher out of tarp and two long poles.

I was finished with my job, but my dad and Andrew were still working, so I stood in front of Coracle with the additional questions I'd wanted to ask. "Coracle, are the people in there really alive?"

"Technically, yes, but they will need forty-eight hours for their internal organs to fully begin operating."

Andrew and Dad finished and came over to join me. They seemed interested in hearing what Coracle had to say.

"One part of the injection your dad gave them is designed to slow down their metabolism since not all the organs and systems get back up to normal levels at the same time. Today your job will be to help them make it to their beds. You will need to help them ingest fluids and maybe a little fruit if they want. My calculations tell me that by this time tomorrow, all three of our time travelers should be awake and somewhat alert. Generally, they will be able to take care of themselves, but mostly they will sleep, drink, and nibble on soft foods. They will seem a little like, how do you say, zombies. They will need one more injection, but tomorrow we can go over what you can expect from the next day on. You have enough to think about with what's in front of you today. Why don't you go bring them to their new resting place?"

We walked nervously down the tunnel to the chamber where we knew that in a few moments we were going to be very close to half-dead zombie-like people. Looking at my dad and Andrew, I could see that nobody was looking forward to this. I decided to take the lead as we approached the first vault where Chief Farquhar lay. I brought the light slowly up his body, making sure I didn't shine it directly into his eyes.

I audibly gasped. His eyes were partially open, and he seemed to be looking around. I could see his chest moving up and down as he took each labored breath. Dad and Andrew joined me.

"Is that the scariest person you have ever seen or what?" Andrew asked.

"I'd go with the scariest," Dad agreed. "From what Coracle said they really aren't awake yet, so we should be able to gently lift them out of the vaults and onto the stretcher without any problems. I'll get the shoulders and you and Colin get the legs." Sometimes it paid to be a kid.

We lifted Farquhar out of his vault and onto the stretcher. We gently carried him through the tunnel and out into the main chamber.

Coracle turned up his lights as soon as we entered the chamber. "Well, if it isn't my old friend Farquhar," he said. Then he spoke a few sentences in a foreign language, which I assumed was Farquhar's native tongue. The chief didn't say anything, although something sparked in his distance stare. Then Coracle spoke to us. "Lay him down on his bed. He will need another liter of water. Colin, come take this instrument out of my side panel and place it over his heart." I took the small gray box and put it on Farquhar's heart as I was told. I looked back at Coracle. "He's a strong one. Yes, I think he will pull through."

After we finished settling Farquhar on his bed, I asked Andrew and Dad if they were ready for number two.

Andrew grabbed the stretcher. "Let's go!"

We lifted out the other two people, bringing them back to the main chamber and making them comfortable in their new home. We each took charge of one person, feeding them small slices of overly ripe fruit and helping them drink water. They didn't have much in the way of appetites, but they couldn't seem to get enough water.

Dad had taken Farquhar, and Andrew had run over to Lachlan's bed, so I was stuck with Effie, but it didn't really matter because they were all the same: silent and nearly lifeless. Still, I had to admit she was pretty. Her curly red hair reached almost to her waist, and she was dressed in a long brown leather skirt and a roughly woven wool sweater. She wore leather moccasins on her feet, and on her hands were leather gloves that didn't quite cover her fingers.

Around three o'clock we realized we were ravenous and stopped for lunch. We ate quickly and in between bites talked about what kind of life these people must have had. How they would react to modern conveniences was just one of the questions we pondered. Coracle entertained us by playing various clips of the tribe in action.

We continued feeding water to our new friends. Then Coracle's lights came on and he spoke to us. "You have successfully completed another stage in the recovery process, and there is nothing more you can do for these people today. You detect that you are mentally and physically exhausted. My recommendation is that you leave now so you are rested for tomorrow's activities."

"Great job, boys." My dad walked over and put his arms around both of us. "Let's do a quick clean up of the area and then be on our way."

Coracle called my dad over and said that the Inventor had left another message for him.

"What? Another letter?" Andrew and I ran over to see what this one said. Like before, a small opening appeared on the side of Coracle. My dad removed the envelope and opened it. He had a strange expression on his face. "There's just one line: 'Always expect the unexpected.' Coracle, why does the Inventor keep leaving me these notes?"

"There is no way for me to know for sure, but I would guess he's challenging you and trying to focus your thinking."

My dad shrugged his shoulders and put the letter in his pocket. We walked up the stairs talking about what the next unexpected event could possibly be. As we emerged from the cave, I was never so happy to smell fresh air and see the sunlight, even if it was fading. When I was younger, I used to make up stories about how great it would be to live deep in a cave, but now that I've been in one, it's not what I'd thought it would be.

On the ride home, I turned to my dad. "What are we going to do with the woman that didn't make it?"

"Good question. Here's what I'm thinking. In a week or two, the others will be up and around, and they should have the right to decide how to handle her funeral and burial.

What do you think?"

We quickly agreed.

That night we hung out in my room, both of us a little sad that Andrew had to go home the following afternoon. It was great having someone my own age around, sort of like a brother. I guess I should be glad that he lived just down the road.

The next day we got up early and traveled to the cave to continue taking care of Farquhar, Lachlan, and Effie. Andrew told me that he hoped they'd start to become more active and alive soon.

"I agree. I'll ask my dad to press Coracle for more details." When I told Dad what we'd discussed, he said he would talk to Coracle again and make sure we haven't missed anything.

He pulled a chair up to Coracle's eye and asked him if everything was all right because there seemed to be no change in their condition. "We're concerned about these people. Yes, they are alive, but they are lifeless. I know how intelligent you are, and you have been one hundred percent correct so far, but there has been no improvement in their condition. That can't be a good sign. We all imagined having conversations with them about what life was like, what they believed in, those kinds of things, and it looks like we will instead be nursemaids to human vegetables."

"You will be talking to them soon," said Coracle.

"When?" I called.

"Very soon," he said.

Frustrated, I checked on Effie again. No change.

"Neil, could you come over here?" A small door opened on Coracle's side and Dad and looked in. "There's a tray with three syringes and a bottle of reddish liquid," he told us.

"It is time for their last injections," Coracle says. The tray slid out.

Dad held one of the containers up to the light. "What does this do?"

"It completes the reactivation process. After you give them the shot, you can go home for the night. They will sleep for many hours, and you should return early tomorrow morning before they awaken."

We nodded eagerly. Maybe it would finally happen. We'd been more than patient.

"Well, boys," Dad said, "it looks like this is the final step in the process. Any of you want to do the honors?" When both Andrew and I shook our heads, Dad moved from person to person and gave them each a shot of the reddish liquid with an enormous needle. I couldn't believe what little reaction each of them had. I'd have been screaming bloody murder. Dad put the syringes back on the tray and put the tray back in the opening, and I knew we were through for the day.

"Well, that's it. Let's go grab our things," Dad said. "Coracle, you're the greatest. See you tomorrow."

Coracle seemed pleased with the compliment.

On the way home, I couldn't stop talking. "Can you believe we are riding in some sort of magnet powered car, after finishing the last step in reviving three people who have been kind of dead for many years ... and I have a new best friend? Thanks for talking me into making this move."

Andrew said that he was also very happy that we moved in. He'd never had a summer like this. My dad was smiling as he parked the car in the garage.

As we walked into the kitchen, he said, "How does this place keep getting so messy? I think we'd better tidy up before Andrew's mom comes over. She may not want to leave Andrew here again."

I knew my dad was trying to motivate us to help. He didn't have to be that sneaky, but I let him think he'd worried us. We got busy washing up, sweeping, and taking out the garbage. Dad said to play nearby until Andrew's mom came to pick him up. Then he cleared this throat. "Oh, by the way, Andrew, if your mom asks, tell her that you and Colin spent most of the time playing together ... kid stuff. Understand?"

"Don't worry, Dad. Andrew and I have worked all that out already."

"Excellent." Dad let out a sigh. "Andrew, Colin I don't like keeping secrets like this, and we will have to tell your mother at some time in the near future. I didn't mind when Colin told you because I inferred from the Inventor's letter that he thought Colin needed someone his age to be with him through this. And I'm sure the secret is safe with your mother, too."

We nodded our heads in agreement. We'd talked about that just the other day. As we turned and went to my room to pack up Andrew's things, I looked back to see my dad at the kitchen table staring into his cup of tea. I think the stress and long hours had finally gotten to him.

Amelia arrived at four-thirty, and after greeting us and giving

Andrew a hug, she and Dad had tea at the kitchen able. She told him about her stay in Oban and all the things she had brought back from her shopping excursions. I heard Dad reassure her that Andrew had behaved himself and that he was a good example for me. When she asked what we did, he responded in a general way. She must have seen the exhaustion in his eyes, for she soon said that it was time to go.

Dad called us in from the living room where we'd been half listening to them as we talked about the fast approaching first day of school. Amelia was already in the car as Andrew walked through the back door to the car. Dad pulled him aside and gave him a pat on the shoulder. "We will try to handle everything without you."

Andrew looked disappointed but offered us a smile and thanked my dad for having him. We stood in the doorway and watched until their car disappeared from sight.

— 15 —

DREAMS ARE FUNNY THAT WAY

I missed Andrew immediately. It was so quiet. I found my dad at the kitchen table sipping a cup of tea. His folder was open to his notes. He looked up and rubbed his eyes. "Are you tired, too, or is my age catching up with me?"

"I'm pretty tired. To tell you the truth, I haven't gotten much sleep the last couple of nights. Glad to hear it's not just me. Hey, Dad, why don't we make a big breakfast for dinner and then watch some TV?"

He thought that was a great idea. After dinner, we fell into our favorite chairs in the living room. We tried to watch the news program, but we kept dozing off. Without much discussion, we said good night and stumbled into our rooms. Within seconds of my head hitting the pillow, I was in another world.

I was having a dream about sailing. The warm sun kissed my face, and the refreshing sea air tousled my hair. A moment later a huge storm appeared out of nowhere, wind shrieking and thunder roaring as lightning streaked the gray sky. I opened my eyes, realizing that the storm was no dream. I listened intently and heard the clanging of garbage cans near the back door. Was it the wind? I looked at the clock on the night table. I couldn't believe I'd slept until ten o'clock. What was that racket?

I jumped out of bed and ran to Dad's bedroom. What I saw frightened me. He was still sleeping. I'd subconsciously convinced myself that it had been Dad outside.

I took a deep breath and walked into the kitchen. I grabbed a broom from the pantry, not sure what I was going to do with it. Still, it was better than nothing. I opened the back door slowly and poked my head out. The garbage cans and lids were all over the lawn, but the wind had stopped. Whatever did this didn't seem to be around, so I proceeded down the steps to put the cans back in place. It must have been a raccoon … or an alien or one of the wee people that Mull is so famous for. I chuckled to myself.

I picked up a lid and went to get the can that had rolled almost to the workshop. That's when I saw her. The village woman named Effie way lying on the ground in the middle of the overturned trashcans. Without hesitating, I ran to her side and put my fingers on her throat. I could feel her pulse, weak but steady, and she was breathing shallowly. I picked her up, surprised how cold she was. Where would I put her? Ah, the overstuffed chair in the living room.

After gently putting her down, I put some blankets from the closet around her, hoping they would get her warm. I was adjusting the pillow under her head when I noticed she had regained consciousness. Her eyes were half-open and she was looking at me blankly. "Can you speak?" I pointed to my mouth. No response. I wondered what she was doing here. How did she find our house?

Realizing she might be thirsty, I went to the kitchen sink to get her a glass of water. I turned to look at her and saw that she was watching me. As I filled the glass, her eyes seemed to widen. She must be very thirsty and weak. I helped her drink the water and went to get another. She finished the second, and I think I saw a little smile. I refilled the glass again and placed it on the table next to her. I started talking to her, thinking she might understand somehow if I said the words very slowly. She reached down into a pocket in her skirt and brought out a folded piece of paper, which she handed to me. It was from Coracle.

"Neil, I am sending Effie to alert you to a troubling development. Everyone awoke early this morning. Farquhar and Lachlan were talking, and then they began fighting. I think it had to do with which man would get to be with Effie. Pushing lead to swordplay and Lachlan was killed. Farquhar was badly wounded. Please return as soon as possible with a needle and thread, bandages, and a disinfectant. Effie will be very tired. Give her lots of water and make a place for her in your house."

Without thinking I ran toward my dad's bedroom. "Dad, you have to get up right now!" I burst into his room.

He sat up groggily, trying to focus. "What's all the yelling about? What time is it anyway?" I tried to remain calm. "It's late. Something woke me up. It sounded like an animal or something knocking over the garbage cans. I came to your room and saw that you were asleep, so I went to investigate myself. Well, Effie was lying there among the cans, so I picked her up and brought her into the house."

Before I could begin the next sentence, my dad had jumped out of bed and was racing to get his pants and shirt on. "Go on! Keep talking!"

I told him why Coracle had sent her here.

My dad was standing in front of me with his shirt buttoned halfway. "Let me see the note." He read it as he ran into the living room to see how Effie was doing. I followed him quietly.

He looked at the woman in the chair and then back at the note. He turned and whispered to me, "This is not good. Two out of the four are dead, and the other two don't appear to be in the best shape. If we try to stay calm and take good care of her, Effie might make it through the day. We need to be strong to get out of this mess, okay?"

"I'm with you."

Dad looked down at Effie again. "Let's put her on the couch where she'll be more comfortable." We made up the couch with clean sheets and blankets. We pulled a small table over next to her and put a large pitcher of water, a glass, and a straw on it.

Dad ran in the bathroom and then outside to the shop to gather supplies. I stood in front of Effie and talked very slowly as I gestured with my hands. "We'll be back as soon as we can."

Once we'd strapped ourselves into the Anti-G car, my dad turned to me, concern shadowing his features. "I guess my doctoring skills are about to be tested." He worked the throttle and the car responded. I'd never seen him go so fast. We arrived at the cave in just ten minutes. As we made our way through the tunnels, he said, "This was not what I envisioned doing today."

I was sweating and cold at the same time as we approached the stairs leading into the main chamber. We were about to find out what was happening in there, but I didn't know if I was prepared.

My dad made his way over to Coracle. Again, I was his shadow. "Where are they? Where is the injured man?"

"Over there." Coracle turned his light on the two men lying on the other side of the room. At first I couldn't tell was alive and which was dead. My dad approached Lachlan; he was covered in blood. Dad felt for a pulse, and I could tell by his expression that there wasn't one. He moved to Farquhar and started to work on him. "He's still alive but unconscious. Coracle, can you give me more light?"

"Yes, of course." The light increased until it felt like high noon.

"That's better."

I felt sick to my stomach. I'd never seen this much blood before, except in the movies. Dad motioned me over and told me to put some water in a bowl and wash the blood from his arm and leg. There were two large cuts. I could see why Coracle had asked for the needle and thread. But would they be enough? After we cleaned and sterilized the cuts, Dad disinfected the needle and thread. He carefully sewed the wounds and wrapped them in gauze.

I rinsed my shaky hands and moved to sit at the table in front of Coracle. Dad joined me a minute later. "Is there anything else I should do for him?" he asked Coracle.

"That is all for now. If he makes it through the day and night, he has a very good chance of surviving."

"So, Coracle, tell us again what happened," Dad said wearily.

"It was eight o'clock, and all three of the people were up and walking around. It was sooner than I'd predicted. It seemed that the chief looked around and couldn't find Ister, so he walked over to talk to Effie. She didn't say anything but just sat there looking miserable. Then again, she hasn't spoken one word yet, so it probably makes her uncomfortable. Sore throats are a natural side effect of not speaking for so long. Anyway, Lachlan came over immediately, and the two men began talking heatedly. It wasn't long before the chief threatened Lachlan, and they began fighting. Farquhar is very accomplished with his sword, and he soon eliminated Lachlan ... but not without taking a few shots himself."

"They both must be very strong to wield those heavy swords in their weakened state," I said.

"Yes, and it was the chief's direct hit to the midsection of Lachlan that killed him. Then it was up to Effie to get a message to you. The map I gave her must have been accurate. But the fact that she had the strength to walk to your house is amazing."

Dad was rubbing his head. "All of us had hoped for a much different outcome. Maybe if we had stayed the night here, we could have prevented this."

"If you had, you would surely have been killed along with Lachlan. My experience with this group of humans is that when in doubt, you kill now and ask questions later. Is Effie resting right now?"

"Yes."

"I would suggest you go back and attend to her. There is nothing you can do here until tomorrow."

I could see that Dad was more than happy to take Coracle's advice. "Colin, come help me lift Lachlan onto this tarp. We need to wrap him up."

I walked to the feet of Lachlan (there was no way I was taking the head) and got my first good look at him. He was short with long, straight brown hair. His features were finer than the chief's were, but he was dressed in the same type of clothing. He still had a sword clutched in his right hand.

On the count of three, we lifted him to the middle of the tarp, which was spread out on the floor next to his body. I let my dad do the wrapping and securing with rope. "Dad, are we going to bury him?"

"When Effie is stronger we will ask her if there is a special way that burials were done," Dad said. "Oh, by the way, Coracle, when do you think she will start to speak?"

"Her voice should be back in less than a day," Coracle replied.

"I wish we understood the language," I said with a sigh. We have no idea how to ask her even the simplest things. Do you have a dictionary or something?"

"I guess that could present a problem," Coracle said. "This may help. I used it with another tribe long ago. Let me reprogram it." A few seconds later, a door opened on the side of the ship. Inside was an earpiece and a small box. "Using this will allow her to understand you and for you to understand the Pic language. Basically, you'll be hearing the responses in English."

I picked up the equipment and put the earpiece on; then I asked Coracle a few questions to make sure I knew how to operate it. I studied it carefully, trying to figure out how it was made. Everything seemed molded as one piece, with no screws or seams. I looked up at Coracle. "You are a very incredible entity," I said.

"Thanks for the compliment," Coracle replied.

"Dad, this will really come in handy. I can't believe how light it feels. I'd never seen anything like it." My dad took it and looked at it closely, turning it over as I had. Coracle projected an image on the wall of a human with a big goofy smile. We all laughed and for a brief moment were able to forget why we were there. We packed up the things we needed to take home and left the cave with lots to think about.

On the way home, I tried to dispel the image of those two men lying in blood. Dad didn't say much about what we had just done, but I knew he was thinking about it, too.

We parked the car and Dad said he was going to put some stuff away and then run out for a few things we would need tomorrow. I told him that I was going to see how Effie was doing. He nodded his head in agreement.

I leaned my head against the back screen door and listened without going or looking in. I was thinking she might be waiting for me with one of our kitchen knives. I told myself I was being paranoid, but my heartbeat quickened when I heard water running at the kitchen sink. It stopped and then I heard footsteps walking away. Wow, she recovered fast. She could barley move only a couple of hours ago. These people are so strong they're scary. I waited a few minutes, but there weren't any more sounds.

I quietly pulled the door open after taking off my shoes. Stepping heel to toe through the kitchen, I stopped every few seconds to listen and look around. There was no sign of anyone. I continued through the kitchen door and into the living room. And there they were.

I announced myself. "Andrew!"

He quickly jumped out of his chair, spilling the glass of water down his shirt.

"Colin, you nearly gave me a heart attack."

I decided there was no need to confess that I was the one that was scared. "Sorry, but I couldn't help myself." I laughed at his expression. "I see you found our new houseguest."

"I was knocking on the front door and no one answered, so I thought maybe you were still sleeping. I thought I'd wake you up." Andrew had the decency to look sheepish after just walking in. "The back door was open. When I came in and found Effie lying here all by herself, I thought you and your dad might have been kidnapped or something worse. But then I found the note Effie brought. She woke up and looked like she wanted some more water, so I decided to watch her until you got back." He paused and ran his hand through his hair. "I was starting to get worried. I didn't know what I was going to do if you didn't show up soon. So what does it look like at the cave?"

We went into the living room and I filled Andrew in on all the gory details. Effie abruptly opened her eyes and looked around. "Andrew, Coracle gave me this," I said, pulling out the translator. "Might as well try it out." I put on the earpiece, turned the switch, and said to Effie, "Is there anything you need?" I hadn't really expected an answer, so I was shocked to hear her voice in my earpiece.

"Is he alive?"

"You can speak and understand me? This thing really works!"

"Yes, I can," said Effie.

"Were you talking about Lachlan?" I knew she was, but I quickly glanced away, not sure how to tell her the bad news and not wanting to seem like I knew too much.

"Yes," she said softly. I knew then that she already knew. She just wanted confirmation.

I hung my head. "I'm sorry to say he is dead ... and Farquhar is in very bad shape. Coracle says if he makes it through the night he has a good chance of surviving."

"That animal should die," whispered Effie, staring at me with those piercing green eyes. She then told us that if she had known what was going to happen to them when they awoke, she would have preferred to fight and die in her own time.

"Was Lachlan your husband?" I asked.

"No, but we were in love and hoped to be married sometime in the future."

Andrew sat in the chair watching and trying to follow what we were saying. I repeated everything Effie had said.

This was a sad situation; we were going to have to watch Farquhar closely. I thought Effie looked scared, so I pulled a chair over and sat down next to her. "You will be safe here. There is no way Farquhar can make it out of that maze of tunnels, much less find our house!"

Effie cocked her head and fingered a necklace I hadn't noticed before. It was made of colorful stones and seashells. I noticed her hands were shaking. "You should not underestimate what can or cannot be done. The proof is lying here in front of you."

I knew she'd put me in my place. It was time to change the subject. "Is there anything you want ... food or water?"

"Do you have any fruit or berries?" she asked hopefully.

"We have apples and pears. Be right back." I got up from the chair and started toward the kitchen. "If you need to use the bathroom, it's down there." I pointed down the hall.

"What is a bathroom?" she asked.

I pointed to my crotch. It's where you go to ... well ... go. You know, pee? Probably very different than what you are used to. Andrew and I can help you walk down there." When I saw that she was trying to get up, I ran to help her. I put her arm around my shoulders and walked her slowly down the hall. Andrew was right behind us, ready to catch her if she fell backward. He didn't seem to want to touch her otherwise.

"Okay," I said, lifting the toilet lid. "Just sit here and when you have finished going, use this paper for wiping. Then push down on this lever and the water will take everything away."

She said that this toilet was unbelievable and wanted to know how it worked. She'd looked around in fascination as they'd walked down the hall. "There are so many things that I want to know about."

"Sure, I will be happy to answer any of your questions," I said.

She told us that we were very kind and that she appreciated what we were doing for her. "I will use your ... bathroom now."

"Fine. Andrew and I will get the fruit for you. Just call when you are finished, and we will help you back to the couch." I turned to Andrew as we were walking down the hall. "The next thing I'm introducing her to is the shower."

Andrew smiled. "Thanks for taking the lead in helping her walk."

As we approached the kitchen, I saw an envelope on the coffee table. I picked it up. "Oh, I forgot to tell you it's a response from the bottle we threw back into the ocean." We had added my address to our note. "It's from a family that lives on the island of Colonsay. They said that they added their name to the message in the bottle and threw it back in the ocean. They asked what kind of things we were doing to keep busy this summer." We had a good laugh over that one. As if anyone would believe us!

We talked about where we thought the bottle would turn up next as we were preparing fruit for Effie. Dad walked in and I filled him in on what had happened with Effie and showed him the letter. Effie returned from the bathroom, and the four of us spent the next few hours in the living room. We talked about basic things, such as how machines weave our cloth. Effie asked about lights, and we showed her other appliances and kitchen gadgets. From the questions she asked, it was apparent how intelligent she was. Once you explained things to her, she was quick to understand.

This is what I had hoped would happen with these people. I looked over to see my dad smiling. He was using the translator now and having a lengthy conversation with Effie. I hadn't seen him this relaxed in a long time. Of course, we hadn't yet faced the next big issue: the chief. How would he fit in once he healed and calmed down?

When it was time for Andrew to go home for supper, he stopped at the door and turned to me. "My mom said I have to work around the house tomorrow, and the next day we are going into town to visit some of her friends. They have a younger boy I'm supposed to play with. Sorry I can't help out with things here."

"That's okay," I said, trying to conceal my disappointment. "Just come over as soon as you can, and I will tell you everything that happened." Andrew nodded. I had a feeling there was more to Andrew not being able to come over than he said. If he really wanted to, he could have made up an excuse or something. I think he was having a difficult time adjusting to all that has happened. It would be good for him to have some time to think about everything. Then again, it would probably be good for me, too.

Dad, Effie, and I had a simple dinner of pork chops, rolls, canned peas, and ice cream for dessert. I'm not sure if Effie liked everything, but she ate it. I think the ice cream was her favorite. As she cleaned her bowl, she kept yawning and looking longingly toward the living room. She began trying to tell us something about Lachlan, but passed out in her seat before she could finish what she was saying. After we put her back on the couch, Dad and I cleaned up and were in bed in less than twenty minutes.

— 16 —

GRAVE DIGGING? YOU'RE JOKING!

A hand was shaking my shoulder. I opened my eyes, startled to see the face of a strange woman speaking gibberish. For a moment I didn't know where I was or who this person was. But I quickly started to come around and realized it was Effie. She handed me the headset and I turned it on.

"What is it?" I asked. The sun was barely up.

"We need to go back to the cave and bury Lachlan. Please. Time is running out. We have to bury him before the sunsets today. His soul will have a difficult time ascending if we wait too long. I am feeling much better and will help you."

I studied her. She did seem stronger. Perhaps the meal had fortified her. "All right. Let me talk to my dad." I walked down the hall to his room and knocked.

"What?" His tone told me I'd better have a good reason for waking him up so early.

I opened the door and sat down next to him on the bed. I told him what Effie wanted to do. "She says we need to do it before tonight or his soul won't ascend. Something like that."

He sighed and threw back the covers. "Let me get ready then."

I went back to Effie and asked if she wanted to take a shower and clean up.

She said no, that she was fine. I knew I'd have to insist after we returned. Years of not bathing had a way of catching up with someone.

I went back to my room and got dressed, and we all met in the kitchen for a quick bite. Effie and I were cleaning up the dishes when Dad said, "You've done a great job, son. You two load up the car, and I'll meet you out there in a minute. I still have a few things to gather."

I knew he needed to bring some medical supplies for Farquhar, and he didn't want Effie to know. Effie and I grabbed the sack lunches, and we headed for the garage. I tried to explain to her about machines that moved us around, but I don't think she understood.

Beside the car were some shovels and other things Dad had left for me to load. I put them in the trunk, watching Effie out of the corner of my eye. She was obviously wary of the car. She stood a good distance back from it, looking at it as if it were dangerous. After a moment she stepped forward and ran her hand along the window.

I opened the back door for her and told her to get in and sit down. When she looked at me questioningly, I reminded her that its purpose was to move people from place to place. "Like a horse or a boat, it will take us to the cave."

She slowly moved toward the open door, put her head inside, and looked around. I heard her sigh as she sat down on the seat. After I closed the door, she held tightly to the door handle.

"Don't be afraid," I said, opening the front passenger door and jumping in.

Dad walked through the door with a bag of things for Farquhar. He opened his front door and handed me the bag. Looking back at Effie, he smiled and told us to hold on. The car sailed smoothly out of the garage.

I turned to check on Effie. She didn't seem as nervous. In fact, I think she was enjoying the ride. "We'll be there in a few minutes," I said.

"What is a minute?"

I pointed to my watch and said, "It's our way of dividing time into pieces. We have seconds, minutes, hours, days, weeks, months, and years ... in that order. Each is longer than the one before." When I saw her confused look, I told her we'd talk about it some other time. I didn't want to overwhelm her with too much in one day. And this one had just begun.

She looked out the window and said, "It took me so long to walk this far."

I grinned at her. "Machines rule."

Effie looked at my dad. "Do you have a wife or ... woman?"

"No. Colin's mother died when he was born."

"Yes, that does happen," she said.

I waited for her to ask other questions, but she just looked out the window. I guess her thoughts were elsewhere.

When we reached the cave, Dad parked the car and he and I got out.

Effie waited a moment before opening her door. Walking away from the car, she circled the area. She stopped and pointed. "This will be a good place to bury Lachlan and Ister." She bent down and started throwing dirt in the air. Then she began chanting something I couldn't understand even with the translator. She finally stopped and motioned me over with her hand.

I glanced at Dad. He just shrugged; he was as confused as I was.

I walked over to Effie and saw that we were standing near a small ledge. There was level ground just below the rocks. A couple of trees grew to one side, and there was a nice view of a small valley below. "Here is the place."

She stared into the sky and then turned around a couple of times. "Yes, this will do," she said.

When I told Dad what she'd said, he pulled three shovels from the car, and we began to dig. Once below the grass, the soil was sandy and the digging was easy. I looked over at Effie frequently to make sure she was all right. Although very thin, she was also tall and strong. Not to mention determined, I made sure she had plenty of water. Every few minutes she broke into a chant like nothing I had heard before. She had a wonderful voice.

After we finished digging both graves, we all walked back to the car and had some lunch. With only a light breakfast, we were famished. The way Dad stood up after eating let me know he was taking charge. That was fine with me. He grabbed the stretcher we had used before, as well as some bags of supplies.

Dad asked me for the translator. He put it on and looked at Effie. "You can stay up here and wait for Colin and I to bring up the bodies."

She must have protested, because Dad told her there had been enough violence already. He then relented. "Do you promise not to attack Farquhar?" He looked down at the small knife in the holster she wore around her waist.

Effie nodded, but she was looking at the ground.

"Okay, let's make our way down there and get Lachlan and Ister."

As we started the trek through the maze of tunnels to the main chamber of the cave, I wondered if wrapping up Ister would be messy. Would her arms and legs come off? I thought about how a letter to my mates would sound. I'd helped bring dead people back to life. I'd dug two graves and picnicked with a woman who was over a thousand years old. Now I was preparing to drag two dead bodies out of a cave and bury them. Just another ho-hum day on Iona. I had to laugh. Dad looked at me strangely. I really should pay better attention to the stairs we were descending into the main chamber.

Coracle greeted us in his usual fashion, and Dad and I replied, "Good morning, Coracle."

"Effie, how are you feeling and what do you think about the twentieth century?"

I turned to look at her, but she wasn't there. "Oh, no! Dad, Effie is gone!" Then I noticed that the earpiece and fallen from his ear and now dangled by its cord around his neck. I pointed, hand trembling. He set down the items he'd been carrying and ran around the corner to where we'd left Farquhar. I followed.

Effie was bent over Farquhar and screaming something none of us could make out. She had his sword high above her head and was about to plunge it into his chest.

My dad dove at her and knocked her over. The sword shattered on the ground, just missing Farquhar. My dad hastily stuck the earpiece back in his ear and grabbed her arm. "You cannot do this!" he told her. "We have different ways of dealing with justice and punishment."

She stopped struggling, no match for Dad's strength. He helped her up, and we walked her over to Coracle. We put her on a chair in front of him. Dazed, she stared into the eye and didn't move.

We quickly went back to Farquhar. He was alive but very weak. His eyes met mine, and I didn't know whether he was going to make it. He was almost dead, but Dad told me later that he felt strangely drawn to him and could definitely feel his power.

Back in the main chamber, I could see that Effie was starting to calm down. She was staring at the prone body of Lachlan, and I was suddenly grateful we'd wrapped him up.

I asked Dad for the translator and put in the earpiece. "Listen," I said soothingly, "we are here to honor and bury the dead, not to even the score." I told her that although she had a good reason for what she almost did, we'd have to decide what to do with the chief after we finished the burial. Hoping my approach would work, I waited for her response.

She looked at me with tears in her eyes. "You are right. Let's prepare the bodies."

I gave Dad a thumbs-up, and he patted me proudly on the shoulder. We then lifted the body of Lachlan onto the stretcher while Effie watched sadly. She followed us as we started up the stairs. It was tough going, but eventually we reached the entrance to the cave. We breathed deeply of the fresh air. Carrying a dead guy wasn't exactly a pleasant feast for the nose.

We lay Lachlan in the freshly dug hole and told Effie to begin the burial process while we went back to get Ister. Effie was looking at the tied-up bundle that was Lachlan, the tears now running down her face. I could tell she wouldn't give us any more trouble today.

Dad and I made our way back through the tunnels and quickly

bundled her in the same way we had Lachlan. The odor was overpowering, but neither of us commented on it. I tried not to gag as we began the tedious process of getting the body through the winding passageways. Within a couple hours, we'd buried both bodies.

Effie began placing rocks of different sizes in a pattern on top of each grave. I made a mental note to ask her later what it meant. Right now she needed a moment to mourn.

"It's time to go," Dad finally said, stretching his arms high above his head. "We can come back tomorrow if you want."

I told Effie, and she nodded. None of us said a word during the ride home, and we made our way silently into the house. A moment later, Dad predictably headed for his shop.

Effie was sitting on the couch staring at her lap. I offered her some hot tea.

"I've never had tea, but I will try some."

I brewed a fruity type and brought us each a cup. We sat sipping our tea and staring at each other. Finally, I broke the silence. "I have never been around dead people before. In fact, I've only seen two dead people in my whole life." I didn't need to tell her whom I was talking about.

Her eyes met mine. "I have seen many … too many." Her eyes went blank, and I could tell that she was thinking about something important. "I feel lost in this place," she said, looking around the living room. "I have no idea what most of these things are, how they were made, or where they came from. You get your food out of little packages; I haven't seen you go hunting or fishing once. How can that be? And now my partner is dead and buried. In the past, if there were problems, things I couldn't understand, Lachlan and I would talk about them. I would always feel better. Now there is no one. I just don't know what I'm going to do."

"It must be quite a shock for you, being torn away from everything and everyone you have known. Sometimes I pretend it was me transported back hundreds of years, and I don't know if I could survive."

She stared at me. "A lot has happened since we went to sleep," she said.

"Yes, there are many things that have improved, making life easier."

"That seems to be true. But what am I going to do? How will I live?"

I didn't want her to worry about that right then. "You can stay here. There is plenty of room, and Dad and I can teach you what you need to know to survive and succeed in this time."

Although she looked doubtful, she thanked me for my kindness. I noticed that she was slumped over and definitely in need of rest. I covered her with a blanket and took her teacup. "Get some rest." Her eyes slid shut before she hit the pillow.

I went out to the garage to see how Dad was doing. He was looking over the latest invention, but I could tell his heart wasn't in it. "Just came to unload the car," I said, sensing that he wanted to be alone. When I was done, I headed into the house for a hot shower.

I turned on the fan and started the water before undressing. I stepped into the shower and smiled as the water soothed my tired muscles. I was shampooing my hair when I had an eerie feeling that somebody was watching me. I rinsed my face and saw Effie standing just outside the transparent shower door.

I quickly turned my back, hoping she hadn't seen me naked. "Later!" I motioned her away, not realizing for a moment that I didn't have the translator on. Still, she must have sensed that she'd done something wrong, for she quickly disappeared.

I hastily finished my shower. I felt a little guilty. She was probably just curious. I doubted she'd ever seen a shower before. One thing I knew, whether she wanted one or not, she would be introduced to ours tonight.

She smiled shyly when I returned to the living room. I ran a comb through my damp hair and put the translator back on. "Would you like a shower now?" I asked.

She nodded eagerly. In the bathroom, I showed her how to turn the warm and cold water taps on and off. It was as if I were explaining it to a child. I handed her a bar of soap and a bottle of shampoo and told her how to use both. She just looked in disbelief and wonder. I put a pair of my baggy sweat pants and a T-shirt of Dad's on the counter. "You can wear those when you're finished. Before you get in the shower, please throw your dirty clothes in the hall. Enjoy your shower."

I waited outside for her dirty clothes and ran to the washing machine with them. Leather or not, they were being washed. I added some soap and put them on the delicate cycle.

Dad and I were in the kitchen talking when she walked in an hour later, wearing our clothes, her hair wrapped in a towel. "I think the shower is my favorite thing in this house," she said.

"We're happy you like it," I said. "Come have a cup of tea with us."

"Sure, but I feel very weak, so I won't last long." She sat gingerly on the chair next to me.

"I think we all feel a little weak," I replied. "It was a very intense day." Dad got up to fix her a cup of tea.

"Effie, would you mind if I asked you a question about the burial today?" I asked shyly.

"No, go right ahead."

Dad placed her tea in front of her. She thanked him.

"I noticed that you arranged rocks on top of Lachlan's and Ister's graves, and I wondered what it meant."

"Well, I'm not totally happy with how it looked. The village always collected and stored rocks for burials, but I had to make do with what I could find. But I guess that's not your question. See, each family in the village had its own sign. Lachlan's looked something like a deer. That symbol is always placed on the lower half of the grave. We believe that our inner light travels to the stars. A small chimney is built over the heart to guide the soul to the heavens. We can talk with and give messages to our dead for two days, but after that time, the communication is broken." She bowed her head and stared into her cup of tea. "I was performing Lachlan's favorite songs and chants."

"Thanks for explaining," I answered, translating for Dad. She was still having a hard time over losing Lachlan.

"I'm feeling very tired. Thank you for the tea, but I think I will need to say good night." She put her cup in the sink and walked to the couch.

"You're welcome, Effie," I called. "By the way, Dad says he and I will be going to the city tomorrow to pick up some of our things that were shipped from our last house and lost." She stepped back into the kitchen doorway with a confused look on her face.

"We are going to leave for a few hours in the morning," I said. She nodded and returned to the living room before I could finish. Within a minute, we could hear heavy breathing.

Dad looked at me and shrugged. "I guess she fell asleep. We can go over all the details with her tomorrow."

"I can't believe the trucking company misplaced those boxes during the move," I said. "You know, Dad, there are a lot of toys in one of the boxes. Maybe I can teach Effie to play Monopoly."

Dad just smiled and told me that he would finish cleaning up the kitchen while I got ready for bed.

— 17 —

THOSE SCARY EYES

The next morning at breakfast, Dad and I told Effie to spend the day resting. Handing the translator to her so she could understand the words, we then introduced her to the TV. She didn't seem to like it. She said the images were moving too fast for her, and she worried that what was on the screen was going to come out of the box. It took awhile for her to understand that it couldn't.

The subject matter was another issue entirely. I turned on a movie that had a car chase in progress, and there was a crash. When the people were hurt, she was extremely upset. I had to tell her repeatedly that it was not reality, just fiction.

When I showed her how to turn it off in case it disturbed her, she wanted to understand where the picture went when it was turned off. I'd thought I was finished explaining, but she kept asking questions about how it worked. When I told her that it was hard to explain in detail because I don't know how parts of the broadcast process worked, she looked at me as if I were crazy. How could I use something and have no idea how it works? I told her that's how it is now. We don't have to know.

I started to explain that it would be good for her to see what some of her new world was like, but I could hear Dad honking the horn from the car.

"I have to leave now, but I want to hear all about what you learned and what your favorite program was when I get back." She was immediately transfixed to the screen.

As I got into the car, my dad asked if there was a problem with the television.

"No, it just took Effie a little while to understand how it worked. Everything is taken care of."

"Good. Then let's go pick up our things. The faster we leave, the faster we can get back." I wished we could take the Anti-G car; the trip would take half the time.

As we pulled up to the ferry office, we saw that the ferry that had brought our boxes was just leaving. We were right on time. Although the ferry station was modern, if you looked closely at the building, you could see that the foundation was very old. The wooden structure was resting on large blocks of hand-cut stone. Andrew had told me that the site was originally built over one thousand years ago, but no one knew what it was used for. I should ask Effie if she knew.

My dad handed the clerk a piece of paper, and a side door opened a minute later. A man wheeled out three large boxes. "Where is your car?" he asked.

We helped him put them in the trunk. After thanking him, we were back in the car. I turned to Dad and said, "I wonder how Effie is doing. You know, it's nice having her around. I hope she gets to stay."

"I feel the same way, but we're going to have to come up with a story about who she is and where she came from. I don't think anyone would believe the truth. I can just hear people laughing if we say that she was in a cave after being put there by alien intelligence." I smiled.

Dad started the car, and we began our drive back to the house. We were discussing which room Effie should have and how we could fix it up; we couldn't keep her on the couch much longer.

"You know, Dad, we are going to have to deal with Andrew's mom eventually. You can't expect Andrew to keep this a secret from her forever."

"You are right, Colin. I've been thinking the same thing. I just haven't figured out how or when to do it."

We eventually went back to talking about the room arrangements, but that discussion would have to wait. As we turned on the road to our house, Chief Farquhar was standing in the middle of the road, sword in hand. He wasn't looking very happy.

Dad stopped the car about ten feet in front of him. "What the blazes is he doing here? We have to get him off the road and out of sight. What if he attacks or kills an innocent person?" Dad opened the door, got out slowly, and walked within a few feet of the chief. Dad opened his arms with his palms facing up. "It's me, remember? I helped you with your wounds in the cave. Don't you recognize me?"

Farquhar just stood there, his eyes as vacant as if he were frozen.

Dad turned back to me and said calmly, "Scoot over to the driver's side, put the car in gear, and keep your foot on the brake. If he makes a menacing move toward me, step on the gas and knock him down."

I nodded my head. I'd never driven a car before, with the exception of the Anti-G, and I sure hoped I didn't have to now.

My dad was walking backward to the passenger side of the car. I could see the chief's mouth move, but I don't think any sound was coming out. My dad opened the back door and pointed inside. He then stepped away and tried to show that we were friendly. "Come get in the car." He pointed again to the car door. "Get in so we can take you to a safe place."

Farquhar dropped his sword. It made a clanking sound on the road, and he fell to his knees, his hands grabbing his side. He'd passed out in the middle of the road. I jumped out of the car, and Dad and I ran to him. Dad felt for a pulse on his neck. "He's alive. Looks like we'll have to carry him into the car. You take his feet, and I'll grab his shoulders."

"God, he's heavy," I said.

"Yeah, I know." My dad was puffing.

"He really smells." I was trying to hold my breath.

"If you were this old, you would smell too."

The chief slumped over in the back seat, lifeless, and Dad got back in the driver's seat. I held his sword between my legs in the front passenger seat. Examining it, I was amazed at the detailed carvings in the handle. Looking at the imperfections in the steel blade, I was sure I could see scenes of past battles in my mind. There seemed to be some kind of power coming through it.

"Colin, are you okay? Are you daydreaming? Maybe you should put that down. We're almost home."

"Just looking at the workmanship," I finally said. But it was more than that. This sword had a distinct power, and I wondered if Coracle had something to do with it.

As we pulled into the driveway, Dad turned to me and whispered, "I'm going to stop next to the back door. Jump out and put the boxes next to the door, then we'll drive to the back storage building and drop off our passenger."

I did as he asked, putting the boxes next to the door as fast as I could, then jumping back into the front seat. When we reached the back building, I jumped out again and opened the large doors. I closed them as soon as the car was inside.

"We will make a place in the back room for Farquhar. I don't think he will be going anywhere for a couple of days. We will use that time to figure out how to keep Effie and Farquhar apart."

Could things get any more complicated? My dream of sitting around talking with these people and starting a historical village was turning into a bad dream.

We made a makeshift bed and found a chair and washbasin for a darkened corner of the building. Still unconscious, Farquhar's color didn't look very good, but at least his breathing was more regular. We placed him in the bed, covered him with a blanket, and turned on a small light. After closing and locking the door behind us, we walked up the path to the house.

"Did you see the look in the chief's eyes?" I asked. "That's the scariest thing I've ever seen."

"I agree. When I was sewing his wounds, he opened his eyes for a second, and I felt a chill go through my body. He embodies the word warrior. But even though we are both frightened of him, it is important that we outwardly show no fear. He is out of his element; we are in control and have to act that way."

"Okay, I'll try." This wasn't going to be easy.

"I know you know this, but don't say anything about the chief being in the back building. We would have to tie Effie up if she knew he was back there. Don't let the fact that she is a sweet woman fool you. She has been wronged and will take revenge if the opportunity presents itself."

"No matter what happens," I said as we walked up the back steps, "I want you to know that I think this is the most exciting place on earth. I'm glad we came."

My dad smiled, took a deep breath, and suggested we take the boxes inside."

I opened the back door, still being cautious. "It's Colin and Neil!" I shouted. "We're home!" I heard the TV in the living room, so we walked in and placed the boxes on the kitchen floor.

Effie was lying on the couch, books and magazines scattered all around the couch and floor. A local newscast was on the television. Effie looked up from a magazine with a big smile and handed me the translator. "This TV is my favorite thing in the house," she said. "There are so many stories; it just goes on and on." She gestured to the magazines and books. "Will you teach me how to read these symbols?"

"Sure," I said.

"Please turn the TV off now," she said as Dad turned and walked back into the kitchen.

"I hope you don't mind if I keep this headset on, since I don't know the Pic language. Hey, maybe someday you can teach me some words."

"Sure, I'd be glad to." Excitement still lining her pretty face, Effie motioned for me to sit next to her on the couch. "Let me look at you." She took hold of my hands and looked me up and down. "How old are you?"

"Eleven."

"You seem big for your age," she said. "You look very healthy: no scars and you have all your fingers."

I gave her a funny look and she explained. "Where I come from, life was very hard and there was always fighting and sickness. It was common for people to lose a finger or two, and many people died at a young age. I lost both my sons to sickness, and my husband to the sea. And recently, a very good friend." She paused. "Tell me what happened to your mother."

I looked into her eyes, feeling very comfortable with her. I could feel her energy and power, and I knew I had nothing to fear. We were her new family. I told her the story about how my mom died during childbirth. Although I had thought about my mother many times before sitting here with Effie, she made me wonder again what it might have been like with her had she lived. I think I was drifting, lost in the moment, because I suddenly felt Effie shake my arm.

"Let's talk about happier things. How long have you lived here?"

"About three weeks, I guess." I couldn't believe all that had happened in that time.

"Such a short time," she said. "Where were you before that?"

"Dad and I lived on Mull, the island across the water."

"Someday you will have to tell me how and why you moved. Did you know that I lived just over the hills?" She pointed northwest, and then she frowned. "But that was a long time ago. I saw many things on the television today, and I know I have a lot to learn about this time and place. There's no going back to what was. This is my new home, so I decided to try and make the best of my new situation."

We must have talked for hours by the time dinner was ready. After we ate, Effie and I returned to the couch. I looked up to see Dad watching us from the kitchen doorway. He seemed pleased that I liked talking with Effie. And I did. We laughed as we started discussing favorite foods, friends, and everything else we could think of. When I looked up, the doorway was empty. As I suspected, and he later verified, he'd gone to check on our other guest.

Dad said later that he'd hoped Farquhar was still asleep, especially since he didn't have the translator. He'd taken a pitcher of water, some cheese and bread, as well as some fruit. Fortunately, Farquhar was still out cold.

Dad returned to find us playing Monopoly. As he stepped into the room, he said, "I see you found your games in one of the boxes."

I smiled and grabbed the dice. After I moved my token, Effie squealed.

"You landed on my property! You owe me rent for Park Place."

"She catches on very fast," Dad said as I counted out the rent money. "But you two should get to bed. How about finishing the game tomorrow? You can leave it set up on the table.

"Oh, Dad, it's not that late," I said.

"It's after ten. You've had quite a day, and the way it's going, you will probably have another tomorrow. And have you unpacked all the boxes yet?"

"All right," I mumbled, rising. I knew I would never win this argument.

"Come on, Effie. Let's clean up this mess so you have a place to sleep." We left the game on the coffee table but returned the books and magazines to their shelves. "Maybe tomorrow we can clean out the back room so you can move in," I said.

"Really, I'm going to get my own room? That's great!"

I told her good night, happy to see her so happy. "Effie, I am really glad you are staying with us."

"Good night, Colin. Thanks for everything."

I took a quick shower, brushed my teeth, combed my hair, and put on my pajamas. I was in bed when my dad walked in to say good night.

He pulled the covers up to my chin and told me how proud he was of me. He said that there was no way that he could have predicted that we would be in this situation, and he was sorry that I had to see and then help bury those dead people.

"Dad, you're right that it was scary and strange, but what an adventure! I just hope Effie will continue living with us. I really like her."

"As far as I'm concerned, she is welcome to stay as long as she wants to. Tomorrow we'll go to the cave and talk to Coracle. I'm sure he will know the right way to handle our two travelers from the past." He also let me know that it was my job when we were at the cave to keep Effie away from Coracle so Dad could talk to him privately about her.

"Maybe we can explore another tunnel or try knocking a hole in the wall we found a few days ago."

I drifted off wondering what the next day would bring. I knew we only had a short amount of time to figure out how to keep Farquhar under control. No amount of injuries could keep him down for long.

— 18 —

WILL HE STAY OR WILL HE GO?

The next morning Dad had me ask Effie if she wanted to go visit Coracle. I was always using the translator and hated giving it up.

Effie nodded.

I glanced at the calendar on the wall. "Dad, can you believe school will be starting in less than two weeks? Where did the summer go?"

Effie looked at me and smiled. "Where did hundreds of years go?" I told Dad what she'd said and everybody had a good laugh.

"Colin, where is your friend Andrew?" she asked.

He can't come over until tomorrow. His mom is taking him shopping for school stuff."

"Don't ever take him for granted," Effie said. "He seems like a very good friend for you, and good friends are not easy to find."

I nodded, wondering where that had come from.

Dad gave Effie the job of gathering supplies for our trip to the cave. He said we'd be checking on something outside (he winked at me), and then we'd bring the car to the back door. I saw him fill a jar with water and grab some food from the pantry when Effie was in the bathroom. If Farquhar were awake, he would be hungry.

Dad and I opened the door to the back building wondering what we would find. As we slowly stepped into the dim interior, all seemed quiet. We quietly approached the bed. The chief was awake, his eyes open, and we both jumped instinctively.

Dad held out the food and water and said, "These are for you to eat." He pointed to his mouth and made a chewing motion.

The chief nodded his head in acknowledgment as Dad placed the items on a little makeshift table next to the bed. Dad told me that it looked like he had eaten some of the food and had some of the water from last night.

Farquhar closed his eyes and put his head back down on the pillow. It looked like he was recovering. We hurried out of there, not wanting to draw any attention from Effie. She was very intuitive and could sense any small change in behavior. We took one last look as we left the room. In the car at last, we drove it to the back of the house where Effie was waiting.

She jumped in, apparently no longer afraid of the car. She leaned forward and looked into my eyes. "What took you so long?"

"Just cleaning up a few things in one of the buildings. It's been pretty busy lately and there were some things out of place."

"Oh, really," she said.

I hoped Dad would get the ride over quickly. I didn't like lying to Effie. She seemed to sense that things were not right.

Dad turned his attention to driving. He was getting the hang of the car. He pushed the lever forward further than usual and the car quickly lifted off the ground. "Wow, this thing flies like an airplane if you want it to," he said. He eased back the lever, and the car immediately slowed and lost altitude as it came back to Earth. "We'll practice that maneuver some other time."

I noticed Effie clinging to the armrest with both hands. Perhaps I'd been wrong in thinking that she wasn't scared of the car anymore.

When we arrived at the entrance to the cave, Dad turned to Effie. "We put Farquhar in one of the smaller chambers to recover, but I don't want you going after him. Agreed?" Effie nodded. "All right, group. Let's make this visit fun!" Dad put on a big smile.

Each of us took a bag of stuff down the stairs and through the tunnels to the main chamber. I was wondering if it was a good idea to bring Effie along, but what choice did we have? We couldn't very well leave her at home with the chief.

After greeting Coracle and placing our bags on the table in front of him, Dad handed Effie and me a shovel, a crowbar, and a pick. "Why don't you go down the tunnel and start working on loosening the stones in the wall? Colin, fill Effie in on what you found. I will meet you two inside after I have had time to discuss a few things with Coracle."

Curious as to what they would be talking about, I took my time exiting the room. I heard him tell Coracle that Effie and I got along so well together. He was right. With our lights and equipment in hand, we headed down the tunnel, talking and laughing. Sometimes it felt as if we had known each other forever.

"Don't let any rocks fall on your heads," I heard Dad call.

I was chipping away at the wall when Dad approached us about thirty minutes later. Effie had a spotlight focused on me.

"How's it going?" he asked.

"I think I found a loose section up here near the top," I said. I had chipped away handholds and toeholds for climbing to the top of the wall, and that's where I was working when he arrived. I scurried back down the wall and told him that the area above was the only spot that showed promise. "Dad, I think if you give the brick a couple big hits, we can push it through."

Dad grabbed a pick and climbed to the top, asking us to keep the light shining on him. He hit the same spot repeatedly with the pick.

"Try to move it!" I shouted, handing up the crowbar.

Dad jammed the crowbar between the stone and large brick and pulled. There was a cracking noise.

"You've done it!" I cried, nearly jumping up and down. "I saw the brick move. Keep going." The stubborn brick didn't want to give way, but with a bunch of pounding, it eventually fell inside to the floor below. I climbed up and joined Dad at the top. Effie handed me the flashlight so we could see what was inside.

My beam of light lit the small room. I moved it along the floor and each of the walls. The entire room was finished and beautifully decorated with painted murals on each of the walls.

"Look at that wall!" I said. "It looks like the evening sky." I moved my light to another wall. I couldn't figure out what the picture was, but it looked like a round, fiery ball. I moved the flashlight again. "What do you think the people are doing in that picture?" There were two big rocks in the ground, and people were standing around them holding different shaped objects. I motioned for Effie to join us up on the wall. There were three more spots for her to climb up. "What is that?" I asked her when she joined us.

"That's a Shanglang."

"What's that?"

"It's a special type of religious ceremony that happens twice a year. It's a time when our village, along with a few others, gathers to feast, trade, and catch up on news from other villages."

I was listening to Effie explain as I continued exploring the room with the light beam from the flashlight. I moved the light to the floor in the center of the room. "Look!" I shouted. There was a coffin-like box decorated with a series of scenes, all of them with a spaceship as the focal point. "It's Coracle," I said. "Look, it's the ship protecting the village. See, it's using a death ray there and a blinding light there."

"Maybe it's a tribute to Coracle," Dad said. "Let's move more of these rocks and go inside."

We began to loosen and push more stones and bricks out of the way and soon had a hole big enough to crawl through. We went back down the wall and waited while Dad fashioned a ladder out of rope, and then climbed back up to secure it to the top of the wall and push it through the hole we'd made. We took turns crawling through the hole and carefully stepping down the ladder to the floor below. Flashlight blazing, we walked over to the coffin in the center of the room, admiring the workmanship of the box.

"These people were incredible craftsman," Dad said. Look at the detail and precision in the pictures." He ran his hand along a section of the box. "It looks like they melted the color into the small groves in the stone. Come on, son, let's see what's inside."

We each took a side. On the count of three, we lifted the lid. The top wasn't as heavy as it looked. We waited until Effie joined us before shining the light into the coffin.

I heard a collective gasp as we first looked at the body. Effie said something I didn't understand and moved toward the body. My dad grabbed her and settled her down.

"What kind of weird ritual is this?" I wondered aloud. "It looks like they partially skinned the person. Or maybe he just had some serious skin problem." I took a knife out of my pocket and slowly put the tip under a piece of loose skin on the side of the person's face. It lifted right off. It wasn't attached. I shuddered.

"You're right, Colin, said Dad. "Looks like they completely skinned the guy, and then laid his skin back over his body."

I was peeking under the skin to look at the skeleton when I gasped again. As if I'd been shocked, I pulled the knife out, letting the skin drop back into place.

"What is it?" asked Dad.

"I don't think it's human. Look at this." Dad and Effie watched as I again lifted the skin. This time I laid it to the side. We stared at the head and neck. "It's part mechanical and part living. I don't think anyone is born looking like that."

Dad reached up into the skull and pulled out what looked like a small circuit board. He studied it closely. "You know, something about the face seems very familiar to me."

"Dad, don't you think this face sort of looks like the face of Chief Farquhar?"

He nodded quickly and discreetly toward Effie. Her face was tightening up. "We could make up all kinds of stories about this, but I'd rather go ask Coracle what he knows. I have a feeling he can answer most of our questions."

While Effie stared at the creature in a sort of trance, he pulled me aside and told me what he and Coracle had talked about earlier. Coracle had been aware that the chief had left the cave, but there was no way to stop him. "I told him that we found him, and he was recuperating at our house in a back building. I asked what would happen when he got better. Would he try to kill us? He told me that the chief is a very powerful man who is used to getting his way, and if he doesn't, violence is always the next option." Dad took a deep breath. "When I asked what tactic we should use to try to control him, Coracle said to talk to him with this other translator he gave me." He pointed to his head. "I'm to tell him that I am the chief of this area and have saved his life two times–that I am responsible for bringing him back to life. I should say that he owes me his life, and I have learned through talking to Coracle that he is an honorable chief, too. I'm to tell him how long he has been asleep and explain that things are very different than they were in his time, to let him know what a shame it would be to have survived all this ... only to die if he won't listen. As I told you, Colin, it is most important that we always assume we are more powerful and stronger than he is."

I was completely unprepared for what Dad said next. "And get this. He has some of Coracle's altered genes, too." I swallowed thickly, my response stuck in my throat.

We took Effie by the hand and made our way up the rope ladder, back down the wall, and headed toward the main chamber. I could tell by the way Dad strode over to Coracle that that he was going to get to the bottom of this mystery.

We were standing in front of Coracle when Dad said, "Do you know who or what is interned in the coffin down that tunnel?"

Although she wasn't wearing a translator, Effie could understand Coracle. He was able to speak in many languages simultaneously without distracting the others.

"Why, yes," said Coracle. "It's me. Well, parts of me."

"Uh ... can you explain?" Dad asked.

Coracle reminded us that he'd used this location and its people to continue his research on humans. But for a reason that he could not explain, he became very intrigued with how our being warm-blooded mammals affected how we acted and thought. "I wanted to become part of this place and its people, to know how it felt to be one of them.

I had learned many things about the humans of this village, and I took great pleasure in being part of the group."

Coracle said that he watched the challenges of everyday life and witnessed a time when many men wanted to be the chief, and fighting for power became the norm. He was convinced that he could rule and guide the group in a more peaceful and productive way. He believed these feelings were related to his newfound identity and internal vision of himself. Being a part of the village life was a way for him to reconnect with a part of his ancient past. "And then an opportunity presented itself when Chief Farquhar asked if there was a way for him to disappear until the hostilities passed. That's when my plan came together."

"So what we found in that tunnel are the remains of your partially human body?" I asked in disbelief. "You created a part human and part mechanical body so you could walk around and pretend to be the chief?"

"Yes," replied Coracle.

I glanced over at Effie. Her face was extremely pale. I patted her reassuringly.

Coracle said it was the most valuable and exciting experience he had ever had. He told us that we have no idea how lucky we are to be human. He thought that our lack of brainpower was challenging, but the sheer excitement of living day to day was beyond anything that he could imagine. "If your species doesn't destroy itself, you are on an evolutionary path, which in time will rival any in the cosmos. And that includes my ancestors ... and ultimately even myself."

"That's very interesting," Dad said, "but can you continue with the subject at hand?"

Coracle continued, telling us that only a select few had access to the underground chamber. The current chief's pretense was that Coracle's presence was disruptive and unnerving to the common people of the village. "That was not true. My presence was disruptive only to him and his close associates." Coracle agreed to their plan to put him underground, for he knew he could easily blast his way out of there or anywhere else. After he was left in the cave, he waited for an opportunity to take on a human shape and provide a new kind of leadership, one that would be in the best interest of everyone. He decided that if he set a good leadership example, he could change the way people during that time and in the future. It was also during this time that he began to add selective genetic material to more people. Coracle thought that if people's brains were adjusted and their bodies made stronger it would be easier to live peacefully.

"I'm sorry for not telling you the whole story about how the chief and the others came to be here. I feared that you would not be willing to help me leave this place. All of the past Inventors had promised to help in the beginning, but they changed their minds. They didn't want to give up my ability to answer all their questions. I very much want to leave this planet and rejoin my other parts. Could you please put your wants and needs aside and allow mine to be met?"

My dad didn't answer. Instead, he asked a question of his own. "But will you please tell us more about Farquhar and Lachlan? Maybe then we'll know how to handle the chief."

"Well, Lachlan was one of the chief's rivals in the village. The chief came to me for advice about a village issue, and during that conversation, he told me he was tired of fighting the Vikings. The raids were taking a toll on their supplies and their morale. When we discussed the deep sleep, I assured him that during their unconscious state they would gain increased intelligence and physical strength– all included in the special treatment. I'm sure you've guessed by now that the real reason I granted his request was to get him out of the way."

I could see that something had really changed Coracle. Maybe it was just part of his own evolution, but Coracle knew that he was more than artificial intelligence and machine parts. He had taken the step from simply carrying out tasks to having his own thoughts and making his own decisions. Coracle had developed emotions. He wanted to continue his journey with the village, and becoming the chief was the next step to fully experiencing it.

"The problem," he continued, "was that I needed a human to help complete my transformation. So during one of the regular council meetings, I asked Lachlan to stay behind. I told him of the chief's plan to escape and rule again later. Lachlan asked if I could arrange for him and Effie to join the chief after they were both asleep. Lachlan was jealous of the chief's standing in the village, and whatever the chief was doing, Lachlan wanted to do. It was all going as planned.

"After the chief and Ister were asleep, Lachlan helped me take measurements and get other details of Farquhar's body. He also provided me with the body of a recently dead male. As you may have noticed, my body, or ship, has many unique properties. Anyway, Lachlan placed the body of the man inside the ship; I altered his body to suit my needs. I told Lachlan that it was important that the tribe not know Farquhar had disappeared because it could cause the tribe many problems. He agreed. Without his assistance, none of this would have been possible."

Coracle was sure that Farquhar was surprised and confused to see Lachlan when he awoke. And the fact that Ister died during the process was one more reason to make him angry at and suspicious of Lachlan.

I looked at Effie then, wondering what she knew of this. There was very little emotion on her face.

"So the fight the chief had with Lachlan was over more than Effie?"

Coracle conjectured that Farquhar thought he'd been betrayed and had no choice but to eliminate his competition.

Dad broke in. "One more a question. Why do you need us to help you leave? I mean, you have incredible amounts of information about just about everything, including great weapons and power, so why you are still here?"

Coracle told us that to complete his transformation into a human body he'd needed to use parts from his ship's instrumentation, which had weakened a number of his critical systems. The result was that the ship was not able to blast out of the cave. Eventually, Coracle began preparing for the death of his new body. He was training a tribe member to remove the important parts and return them to the ship so he could leave. But this plan was interrupted when a rival member of the village killed Coracle and his assistant suddenly and without warning. Coracle made a critical error when he forgot about the fragileness and unpredictability of organic life forms. He had no one to transfer parts back to the ship. "That is why I need your help."

"I've got a question about the room you were in," I said. "Do the murals on the sides of the walls have any meaning or are they just for decoration?"

Coracle said they all had meaning. During his rein as chief, one of his objectives was to strengthen all current socializing rituals. He felt that people needed a safe place to meet. Moreover, the need to trade was surely greater than the instinct to fight. He said that quite a few of those kinds of meetings already existed, but he added elements that forced many other villages in the area to interact with them. He brought them together in peace under a common theme. "It broke down the natural tension and distrust that existed between our groups and allowed us to focus on our common enemy, the Vikings."

Effie spoke up for the first time. "My favorite ritual was when we all gathered for the Shanglang."

Coracle agreed. "The Shanglang was an existing event to which I added more elements. There's no question that it was the largest and most successful. A scene from that event is pictured on one of the sidewalls. The back wall is an image of what my home planet looks like. I know it doesn't really belong there, but I wanted to leave a piece of my history. I told the villagers that it was a recurring dream that had significance to me. And the other painting is of the land and sky from this very spot–close to two thousand years ago."

Coracle was surprised that we didn't mention his coffin and the scenes depicted there as a sort of homage to him. He told us how he introduced new techniques for making finer tools and gathering and processing materials to make glass. Some of those techniques and materials were used on the coffin.

Coracle said if we had any other questions he would be happy to answer them. Nobody did. He then said that we now knew the whole story, and he hoped we could understand why he did what he did. He asked us again if we would assist him in escaping.

I finally looked at my dad, wondering what he was thinking.

Dad cleared his throat. "Coracle, are there any more frozen or dead people hidden down here?"

"No, Neil. You have found all of them."

Dad was silent for a moment, and I knew he was wondering what to say next. Coracle had provided him with the answers to many questions and ideas for new inventions. Knowing Coracle had given our lives new meaning and purpose; not having him around would be a big loss. Plus, what about the two people he helped us free?

"We will be back tomorrow with an answer. We need to discuss it tonight."

"That seems like a very wise plan," Coracle said.

We gathered our things and said goodbye to Coracle. Just as we were about to leave, Coracle said he had another letter for Dad.

He opened it and said, "Another message from the Inventor."

"Read it out loud," I urged.

He cleared his throat again. "'Your decision to free Coracle will affect many lives. When I was alive, I did not have the courage. Do what you know is right.'"

"It's like the Inventor is inside Coracle," I said. "He seems to know what we are doing, or are about to do, all the time."

"Interesting thought," Dad replied. He stepped in front of Coracle's eye. "By any chance is any part of George Beaton inside you or part of you?"

The light of his eye came back on. "Yes. George's thoughts and memories are indeed inside me."

When Dad asked whose idea that was, Coracle explained that George wanted to experience what it was like to exist as electrical energy, to have endless access to data and information, to live without the bounds of time. He wished to be able to invent and create, not just use Coracle's instructions to assemble things.

"And how did this transfer take place?"

"That was not easy because George had to attach sensors to his head to monitor the downloading of his experience, learning sequences, and personality while leaving just enough of himself in his body to walk back to his house and die where someone could find him. Although it all worked out, as your being here proves, it was still a calculated risk that George wanted to take."

"Can he talk?" I asked.

"No, but he can communicate in writing, as you have seen."

"Can I ask him a question?"

"Not directly. However, if you state your question, he will receive it, and you will have your answer tomorrow."

"Okay, ask him if he is happy with his decision,"

"You will have your answer tomorrow."

"And with that, we left the chamber and walked back to the car. All the way out of the cave, I asked my dad question after question about what he believed it would be like to exist only as thought, without any body. I found it a fascinating concept, but I could see that my dad had other things on his mind.

I decided it was much easier to talk to Effie about village life and the Shangling. As she spoke about her experiences, it was as if I were right there. I wished I had a pen and paper to write everything down. I vowed to do it as soon as we got home.

— 19 —

LAYING DOWN THE LAW AND LETTING GO

Effie and I were finishing the dinner dishes. I'd seen Dad slip out just before we ate, so I knew that he'd given Farquhar food. So what was the hold up? I knew my dad didn't really want to discuss helping Coracle, but we needed to talk about what our answer would be. Finally, I couldn't wait any longer. "Dad, when are we going to talk about Coracle?"

He looked at both of us and said, "Okay, let's each take a few minutes to discuss what we think about helping Coracle escape from the cave." He looked at Effie, and I told her what he'd said.

She said that she felt betrayed by Coracle. She'd slept through hundreds of years, and her man was dead because of him. "He can stay in his cave forever!"

When I translated for dad, there was no need to tell him how angry she was. I reminded him to put on his translator, and then I turned to Effie. "But didn't he protect your village from attacks, provide medicines, and give your people solutions to many of their problems?" I countered. "I don't think that Lachlan's jealousy of Farquhar was Coracle's fault."

Effie didn't say anything. She simply stared straight ahead.

"Yes, Coracle has made some mistakes," I said. "Have you ever made any?"

"Of course," she said.

"So it's not a black or white situation." I couldn't believe she would be against letting him go. If I couldn't change her mind, it would be two against one for sure. I think my dad wanted him to stay, too. I studied her and realized that she was lost in thought.

"Colin, what about you?" Dad asked.

I hung up the dishtowel. "I think we should help him get back to his planet, or wherever it is he has to go. He has been away for a long time, and although some of it was his doing, they treated him like a slave. If he wants to go, we should help him. But you already knew that, Dad." My voice shook with my next words. "The real question is … what do you think about it?"

Dad said that his reasons for not freeing Coracle were selfish. He knew so much, and Dad would love to keep building new inventions with his help. Besides, he enjoyed talking to him. "But after a lot of thought, I think we should let him go if that's what he wants."

I had a big smile on my face when I turned back to Effie. Her expression was blank, as if she'd returned to her formally vegetative state.

"Well, it's settled then," Dad said. "We will get up early tomorrow and go tell Coracle our decision. We will ask him how to clear a way for him to exit the cave. After that we will obtain the necessary equipment and set the date."

Effie turned to me. "Can we play Monopoly now?"

"Sure." We moved into the living room and set the board on the coffee table. "Don't be sad, Effie. Coracle is just a machine trying to be human. He doesn't have all the fine points down yet; he's like a kid who doesn't think things through."

"Let's just play," was her only response.

It was hard to say what Effie was thinking, but I knew she was angry, hurt, and confused about what had happened to her. Time was the only thing that could take care of that. With a huge yawn, she said halfway through the game that she was too tired to finish. After I'd tucked her into her new bed in the back room, Dad took me aside. We were going to visit the chief.

Still wearing the other translator Coracle had given him, Dad grabbed a couple of beers, and we made our way to the back building. He opened the door and turned on the light. We walked to the edge of the bed. "Are you awake?" he whispered.

"Yes," Farquhar replied in a scratchy voice.

Dad pulled a chair up to the bed. I would keep a safe distance for now. "Would like a beer?" he asked the chief, opening a bottle.

"I'm not sure what that is," he said, eyeing the bottle warily. When he saw Dad take a sip of it, he held out his hand. "I am thirsty."

Dad popped the top and handed him the bottle.

He looked at the label and then the bottle. He smiled when he smelled it. He took a sip. "This is very good. We sometimes made a wheat or barley ale if we had a large enough surplus. But, as I recall, it didn't taste anything like this."

"We've made some improvements on the old recipe. I thought you would approve of this." Dad pointed to the bottle.

"How long was I sleeping?" Farquhar asked.

"It's been hundreds of years," I interjected. He looked at me then, either in disbelief or as if wondering where I'd come from.

"With Coracle's help I brought you back to life along with all but one of the others," Dad said. "Ister could not be brought back. Something happened to her while she was sleeping. We don't know what it was.

"After your fight with Lachlan, I tended to your wounds and later rescued you from the road. I have saved your life. I would like to be your friend. More importantly, I am the chief of this area and will work to maintain order. I think you understand the importance of that."

Farquhar exhaled. He seemed resigned to the fact that things were not going to be the same as when he was chief long ago.

"Where is Ister now?" asked Farquhar.

"She is buried near the opening of the cave. Effie and Colin buried her and Lachlan yesterday."

"I want to visit the grave," he said, eyes looking at the floor.

"When you are able to get around, I will take you there."

"Thank you," he said softly.

I stared. He seemed almost human for a second. Dad had better stay on task and keep the upper hand.

Dad obviously felt the same way. "You are living in a different time," he said, looking the chief straight in the eyes, "and your ways of resolving problems are no longer used without resulting in the harshest of punishments. I am telling you this because I am the chief of this village and if you want to survive and prosper, you will listen to me. Do you understand?"

The chief looked at him with those steely eyes and nodded his head. After that exchange, the conversation was much milder. He asked Dad questions about what living was like now, and they talked about what had happened in his village during his lifetime. He said that the Viking attacks had escalated, and the constant state of war had torn apart the fabric of his people and village life.

He asked questions about how armies protected their people now, what kind of weapons they used. He wanted to know about wars and how they were fought. He wanted to know what we used to sail the oceans, along with current fishing techniques. He was most curious about the new things he had seen: paved roads, cars, and the strange metal birds that flew in the air.

After an hour, I began yawning and said I was going to bed. I think they'd forgotten I was there, for Dad suddenly whipped around to look at me.

"Yes, of course. I want you to come over and officially meet Farquhar."

I stepped around to the front of the makeshift bed. "It's good to meet you," I said in a shaky voice. "You seem to be feeling stronger."

"Stronger," Farquhar repeated, studying me.

"Thanks for coming down," Dad said, "but you better get back to the house." I looked at Dad and Farquhar and doubted there'd be any trouble.

"Nice meeting you," I said with more confidence. "I hope we can talk later."

Farquhar nodded. I thought I saw a smile. I left the building slowly to see what they would talk about next.

"You know, Farquhar," Dad said, "Effie is very angry about your killing Lachlan, so I'm asking you to stay here in this building until we work out the living arrangements. There is no need for more violence. I'll bring you more food tomorrow."

I scooted out the door when I heard his chair slide back. As I closed the door, I realized that there had never been a time in my life when we had so little control over what was going to happen next.

Later, Dad stepped into my room to tell me good night. I stopped him as he was leaving the room. "Dad, I'm worried about Effie and the chief getting into a fight."

"I worry about that too, but the chief is still very weak. He won't be leaving the building for a while. I planned to talk to Effie about it tonight. Get some sleep. Tomorrow we're going back to the cave to give Coracle the good news."

Figuring I'd done enough of it lately, I tried not to eavesdrop, but they were sitting in the living room, which was right outside my door. Dad must have awakened her. The only sound at first was their spoons clinking against the insides of their teacups. I reached over and slipped on the translator.

"Sorry to wake you, but we need to talk about you and the chief," I heard Dad finally say.

"What about that pig?"

Dad must have decided to use the heavy-handed approach. Why not? It had seemed to work with Farquhar.

"Effie, you are not in your world. I'm sorry about all the things that have happened to you. They are tragic, yes, but you have to learn to follow the rules of this time. You will not try to take revenge against the chief. Our laws prevent killing.

"Now, as you know, the chief is alive. I'm sure you two will meet sometime in the near future, but you have my word that your contact with him, if at all, will be brief. You don't have to like him; you just can't attack him or try to kill him."

She muttered something I couldn't hear.

"Forgiveness is a very difficult to do, and maybe you never can forgive him. But killing him would make you just as bad as him."

After she muttered something else, I heard Dad's footsteps coming toward the hall.

"We'll talk more about this tomorrow at the cave," he said.

After he'd retreated to his bedroom, I crept to the doorway and peeked at Effie. She was still sitting on the couch, deep in thought. This couldn't be easy for her. Not that it had been easy for the chief either.

— 20 —

FORGIVENESS AND GOOD BEER

The next morning, as we were finishing breakfast, we heard a knock on the back door. When it opened, Dad and I froze with our forks in the air. Did Farquhar get out of the building?

"Good morning!" It was only Andrew, a big smile on his face. "Is there anything I can help with today?"

Dad and I both relaxed, and Effie looked at us strangely. "Sure, help Colin and Effie get our things together," Dad said. "We are going to the cave. You should have Colin fill you in on what's been going on. There are a few things you should know about." And with that, Dad slipped out the back door.

Dad had told me to keep Effie busy until he brought the car from the back building, so I had her go make her bed and get her jacket. While she was gone, I quietly told Andrew about burying Lachlan and Ister, finding Coracle's human skeleton, and coming across Farquhar on the road. I had to cut it short because Effie came back in the room.

"Colin?" she said. "I want you to know that I have thought about Coracle and what I said about him last night. I am still very angry at both him and Farquhar, but I am going to try to forgive them. I'm not sure how successful I will be, but I'm going to try." She paused. "I guess we should let Coracle go."

"That's really good news," I said.

Andrew looked a little shell-shocked; he had only been away a few days, and so many things had happened. I thought it might take him a few minutes to catch up.

I asked Andrew to help Effie gather our things while I went to find my dad. I found him approaching Farquhar with a large box. On top of it was a tray of food. He looked rather uneasy, as if he were entering the cage of a wild animal. Farquhar was trying to stand.

"Looks like you are feeling a bit better." Dad set down his heavy load. He then placed the tray of food on the table.

"I-I'm ready to go," Farquhar said as he fell back into his bed. "Ooooh!" he yelped.

"You still need a couple of days. Take it easy and rest, or you will injure something else. It will take you that much longer to recover. We are going to the cave today, and I will be back to check on you late in the afternoon. Is there anything else you need?"

Farquhar grabbed the empty beer bottle from the night before. "More of these!" he bellowed.

Dad said he would bring more tonight if he rested today.

"Uhhh," Farquhar moaned.

"One more thing." Dad opened the box he'd brought with him. I recognized his old black and white TV that he stored in the garage. He plugged it in and faced it toward the bed. After putting it on the news channel, he handed the translator to Farquhar, and said, "You can see what is going on in the world. I'm certain you will find it interesting. Don't be afraid of images coming out of the screen."

I heard Farquhar mumble that he was afraid of nothing. When I tiptoed away, he was putting the earpiece in his ear. I wished I could be there to see the warrior's face as he watched some of the programs. But that would have to wait; I had to get back to the house before Effie became suspicious.

I ran in the house and grabbed the bag of stuff I'd gathered earlier. A moment later, Dad arrived at the back porch where his three passengers were waiting. Everyone seemed to be in a good mood, including Effie. I told Dad how she had been thinking about Coracle and agreed to let him leave."

"That's great!" Dad smiled at Effie.

As we walked to the main chamber, Andrew and I discussed the latest letter from the Inventor. Andrew said that now his death on the road in front of his house made more sense.

"How is that?" I asked.

Andrew said that he couldn't understand why he was not dressed for walking. He wasn't even wearing shoes. Also, it was weird that his body was taken away so quickly and that there was no service or burial place.

"Hmm," I said, not really listening. I was too busy wondering how the Inventor would respond to our question from yesterday.

As usual when we entered the main chamber, we greeted Coracle and put our things on the table in front of him. Now it was time to give him the good news. On the way over, I'd asked everyone if I could be the one to tell Coracle he was getting his freedom. No one had a problem with it.

I stood in front of the eye. "Coracle," I said.

"Yes, Colin?"

"We have talked it over, and we would like to help you escape this cave."

Coracle almost sounded human as he thanked us. "That's what I hoped for!"

Dad walked over to the eye. "Do you have a plan for how to do it?" he asked Coracle.

"Of course. You will get a printed list of the items needed to get me out of the cave."

"That would be helpful," Dad said. "As long as you're printing things out, there are a couple of projects that the Inventor hadn't finished. Could you give me a printout of the assembly processes and any other necessary notes I might need? I would appreciate it."

"Yes, I will give you the information for completing the last of the inventions. I know George wanted them completed, and he thought you the most capable person to do so."

"Hmm. That reminds me." Dad stroked his chin. "I keep meaning to ask why the Inventor wanted us in the house within two weeks."

"I'd say he didn't want people snooping around before they were finished." Coracle then asked us to bring back the body from the end of the tunnel. There were parts from it that he needed to reinstall before he could begin his journey."

"Sure," said Dad, "but it might take some time. We'll need to make that hole a bit wider to get him out. By the way, Coracle, has the Inventor left me any new messages?"

"Let me check. No, not yet."

"Well, maybe later," Dad said.

Andrew kept asking me questions about what the skeleton looked like. I finally told him to wait a few minutes and see for himself.

After banging and chiseling on the wall, Dad made the hole wide enough to move through easily. Dad had fashioned a crude wheelbarrow, and we handed it through to him once he was on the other side.

It was eerie watching him pick up the metal skeleton. The plastic skin fell off at the slightest touch. Effie said that the glass eyes kept looking at her, but she said it with a laugh. She seemed like a changed person. She didn't seem nearly as upset or angry as she had been.

We helped Dad lift the wheelbarrow through the hole. If the skeleton's eyes freaked out Effie, Andrew was even more afraid. He finally put a cloth over the face. He said he did it to be respectful. Right. I'm a little concerned that all this is too much for Andrew.

We brought the body back to Coracle. He requested that we disassemble various pieces of the head and the chest and place them in an opening on the side of the ship. After we finished giving him the parts he needed, he thanked us and asked us to purchase the other items on his list.

We told him we'd see him in a couple of days and started out of the room.

"Neil?" Coracle called. "I have something else for you." The side of the ship opened to reveal two more translators. "Don't know why I never realized you'd need these."

"All right!" I whooped. I was tired of sharing mine all the time. We thanked him and started out again.

"Wait!" he called.

I wondered if he had learned the emotion of loneliness. He didn't seem eager for us to go. We turned back.

"Don't you want George's answer to your question?"

"Oh, yes, of course," Dad said. As before, a small opening appeared on the side of the ship, but this time I reached in and took out the letter. "Read it aloud," my dad said, imitating me.

I gave him a smile as I opened the envelope and unfolded the letter.

> "Thank you for your concern. It's not easy to answer your question because many of my human emotions don't exist anymore. Whatever made me who I was is still there, but the difference is that I am free of my body and time as you experience it. I gave coming here a lot of thought before actually doing it. My passion was putting things together and seeing them work, and Coracle became my drug. As you know by now, the term Inventor is not exactly accurate; assembler is more appropriate. It's the reason that I, and those that came before me, couldn't bare to release Coracle.
>
> "But you are different. You have just begun to assume the title of Inventor, so the drug has not consumed you yet. Second is the grounding that your son provides. Being where I am now, I am embarrassed that I didn't choose to release Coracle when I was still human.
>
> "And to answer your question, here inside of Coracle, research is wide open and the possibilities involving creative thinking are endless, although my current project involves extending great science to purposeful applications. It's like the saying about the tree falling in the forest. Does it make a sound if no one's around to here it? When I came up with a truly great invention, who

would ever know ... and what would I do with it? You asked if I'm happy. I would say yes. This is everything I thought it would be. And more. I hope this letter answers your question."

"Surprise, surprise. It's signed by George Beaton." I looked up at everyone. "Wow, could this be any stranger? The Inventor decided to transfer the information in his brain into Coracle's computer. Dad, promise me you'll let me know if you start thinking that's something you want to do."

"Don't worry, Colin. Being human, as imperfect as it is, is fine with me."

Once again, we had another interesting topic to discuss as we made our way out of the cave. Andrew seemed a little more comfortable; he was even laughing as we emerged from the cave.

By the time we returned home, it was late afternoon. Andrew said goodbye and that he would be back tomorrow.

After we finished dinner, Effie headed into the living room to watch TV, and Dad asked if I'd like to join him for a visit to the chief.

"Sure," I said. While I guarded the doorway to the living room, Dad quickly gathered dinner and beers for the chief.

Dad slowly opened Farquhar's door and looked inside. The chief was sitting on his bed watching TV. Dad and I approached carefully. Dad set the tray down and adjusted his earpiece.

"Good evening," Dad said. "What do you think of your new world?"

"I don't understand what has happened. Everyone is a shopkeeper. Where are the warriors and chiefs? You seem to have such powerful weapons, but they aren't being used."

Dad pulled a chair up next to the TV. "There are still some chiefs out there but very few. War is not good for business. It's better for everybody if we trade with our enemies. Now the war is fought for people's minds and stomachs."

Farquhar cocked his head. "Minds and stomachs?"

"Oh, you haven't really been out to see what our world is like. I have an idea. Tomorrow morning I have to go to Mull to get some supplies to free Coracle–"

"You're going to free the ship?" Farquhar grabbed him by the shirt. "I need to talk to Coracle before he leaves."

"Okay, okay." Dad pulled out of his grasp with a warning look. "You can see him tomorrow afternoon."

"Good." Farquhar settled back onto his bed and picked at his food. He was excited when Dad opened their beers.

"Anyway, would you like to see what has happened to your world?" Dad asked.

"Yes."

"Do you give me your word that you will behave and not talk or cause a disturbance?"

"Yes." His eyes went back to the TV. He was watching a professional soccer game.

"Then you may go with me to Mull. Do you have any other questions before we leave?"

"Yes, many, but overall I'm very troubled with what I see. Take this sporting contest for instance. Why are there so many rules that keep the team with the ball from scoring? Everyone is missing the obvious ways to score. I fear there is no place for my kind in this world." He looked down sadly.

"You haven't seen the whole world yet," I interjected. "There is a place for everyone in this world, including you."

Dad patted his shoulder. "Enjoy your dinner," he told Farquhar. "I'll be right back with some clothes for our trip tomorrow morning."

As we left the building, I had a sinking feeling about what was going to happen to Farquhar. At the very least, he would have to change his profession. There wasn't much of a need for slash and burn experts.

As we neared the house, we heard some incredible singing. I thought perhaps Dad had picked up some new records, but he looked as surprised as I. Effie must be watching a musical or something. But as we entered the house and went into the living room, we realized we were hearing Effie's voice. She was on the sofa, her back to us. We stopped to listen. It was hard to classify the songs, but I liked them. When Effie noticed us, she stopped immediately.

We talked awhile. Dad discreetly gathered some clothes and took them to the chief. He later told me that he'd asked Farquhar if Effie was some kind of special singer in their village. Apparently, she led all the chants and ceremonial songs.

I was able to talk her into singing one more song. I applauded as she finished. "You are fantastic! You could be a rock star, have your own albums."

"What are you talking about, Colin?"

"Let me show you." I went to my room and brought out the albums of my favorite rock groups. I showed her the covers.

Dad walked into the living room. "Are you going to teach her to be a rock star, Colin?"

"She should be. You heard what a great singer she is."

"That she is," Dad replied. "Colin, tomorrow morning I'd like you to stay here with Effie while I go to Mull to pick up the items we need."

I nodded. I much preferred her company to that of the strange chief's.

"I will leave very early and will be back in the afternoon. If all goes smoothly, there may even be time to drill the holes in the rock for the dynamite."

"That means Coracle could be free the day after tomorrow," I said. I motioned for Dad to sit on the couch next to me. "It's been an unbelievable month, and now a big part of the adventure is about to leave. I know if it weren't for how I felt about Coracle, you might not have helped him leave his prison. I know that it's the right thing for him to leave, but I'm also sad. It's like losing a good friend. That probably sounds silly."

Dad put his arm around my shoulder and we walked to the kitchen where we talked about the importance of not taking relationships for granted. As we talked, we heard Effie trying to sing along to a song on one of my records. She'd actually figured out how to use the stereo herself.

— 21 —

A Trip They'll Never Forget

The morning came quickly. Dad pulled me aside and asked that I come with them.

"I thought you wanted me to stay with Effie."

"How about if we ask Andrew to?" he suggested.

"Uh ... sure. But why do you need me?"

Dad swallowed and shrugged his shoulders. He looked embarrassed. I just think it best to have a backup in case anything happens. You know, safety in numbers."

"I understand."

I called Andrew, and although I woke him up, he said he'd be more than happy to come over.

We finished breakfast and went back to get the chief. I had Andrew keeping Effie busy with video games. I hated to say it, but she was starting to turn into an addict. She could even beat me. At least we didn't have to worry about her noticing our driving off with Farquhar.

As we headed outdoors to the back building, I prayed that Farquhar was in a good frame of mind.

Before we even reached the door, it swung open and there was the chief. He was dressed in a pair of Dad's jeans and a T-shirt. He smelled much better, thanks to the soap and hot water Dad had brought him earlier. I noticed he was wearing a translator, as were Dad and I.

"You are looking sharp," Dad said, and we had to laugh at the chief's expression. You really look like a twentieth century guy. You'll fit in with the rest of us. Come jump in the car so we don't miss the ferry."

Farquhar got in and stared at the seats, windows, control panel, everything. He was speechless.

"How are you doing?" I asked him.

"Fine," he said.

"What do you think of the way we get around?" I pointed to the car and the road.

"It is so fast and for so few people."

"Yeah, there are about three hundred people living on this island, but there are thousands of tourists visiting the chapel near the beach each year. We are on the other side of the island. No one comes over here. Nothing to see, I guess." If they only knew what they were missing.

As we reached the ferry, Farquhar was looking around and muttering things to himself. As we got out of the car, he said, "I know this place. We had many battles here. We beat back the Vikings many times, and over the years hundreds of people fought and were killed." He pointed to the area just up the beach. "Over there is where the ancients held their ceremonies. I'll have to tell you the stories."

The ferry looked like it was getting ready to leave. "On the boat," Dad said. "You can tell us there."

It was about a half-hour journey to the other side. Farquhar stood with us at the rail and told stories of how the Vikings would attack from their long boats using broad swords and other hand weapons. He told us how they dressed. He said they looked like devils with metal headgear. He would study the way they positioned their boats before an attack, the formations they used on the ground. He even followed behind their boats in one of his own and watched as they positioned for an attack on another village. This information helped keep his village safe, along with his secret weapon, Coracle. "Yes, he was the fiercest warrior I ever saw. He used weapons that even you probably haven't seen before." He went on in detail about the weapons and techniques used in close combat, as well as what was done with prisoners. The time sped by.

As we got off the boat, Dad told the chief not to talk, just to watch. We went into the local hardware store and picked up the special rock drill bits and the dynamite we would need to blow the hole in the cave. Farquhar wouldn't leave the knife display case, and he kept asking Dad for a bowie knife he saw there. Farquhar pulled Dad to one side and told him that he had never seen such workmanship. He said the steel looked like it came from the gods. Dad told him he would buy it for him, but he couldn't have it until he and Effie had worked out their differences. Farquhar asked if he could hold it for a minute. He turned the knife around in his hand and flipped it back and forth from hand to hand, staring at the blade. Dad told him to put it away. I could see that it was making people in the store a little nervous.

I smiled and said, "He's from Greenland" as we left the store.

We went to a couple more stores and Dad picked up the items on Coracle's list, along with a few things that we needed at home. We walked by a clothing store and stopped to get some jeans and T-shirts for Effie. She'd grown to love our clothes and wouldn't wear hers anymore. The problem was that we were constantly short on clothes now, especially since she liked to change outfits several times a day. At least she helped with the laundry.

Farquhar and I waited outside, and he did lots of looking around. He didn't talk or do anything that would draw attention to him. After the shopping was finished, we had about two hours before the ferry returned to Iona. Dad took us to his favorite old pub.

Inside, it was dark and smoky with the smell of stale beer in the air. There were half a dozen unsavory characters sitting at the bar. I could see that Farquhar was much more comfortable in a place like this than in a store. I imagined that if he lived here, he would definitely be a regular–one of the salty seafaring men who inhabited these parts.

We choose a table in the back corner where we could people-watch without anyone observing us. A server came by, and we ordered drinks and sandwiches. When she left, Farquhar told Dad that he liked the look of that woman. Dad turned to him and gave him the eye he usually gave me when I'd said too much. I was having a hard time keeping a straight face.

I was curious. "So what do you think about how your village area has progressed."

Our drinks came, and the chief grabbed the pint glass, drinking most of the ale in one swallow. He wiped his mouth and said the machines are what have changed. "They have taken over. It seems the machines are more important than the people using them. Like I said before, everyone is a shopkeeper. And there seems to be way too many rules. Your life is spent trying to understand the rules and obey them. Although you do have the most delicious beer I've ever tasted … I can't believe it's real." He drank what was left in the glass and motioned for another.

"I can see that your lives are much easier. People spend time in their heads and not their bodies." Farquhar had me nearly hypnotized. He was intelligent and insightful, and he had that indefinable power that great leaders have. But I knew that just under the skin lurked a cold-blooded killer.

The one thing that Farquhar lamented was the fact that he was the chief of such a small village. When he was alive, the world was there for the taking; the Vikings knew it and they acted on it. "Although they are gone as a group, I just have to think that their influence and people are all over the world. I can see resemblances in people's faces here and on the television. Different opportunities present themselves based on the time you live in. I missed it during my time, and I'm not interested in being a shopkeeper now.

"Thinking back, I remember how jealous I was of the Vikings' power. More than one time I caught myself daydreaming about joining their side, but that would not have been possible."

We continued talking about the differences between daily life on the island now compared to hundreds of years ago. Dad looked at his watch, and I knew it was time to get back to the ferry.

Again, Farquhar marveled at the size of the ferry and its speed. He remarked that if he had had a ship like this one back then, history would have been changed forever.

"That's why these machines are so important to us," Dad told him.

As we were loading our purchases into the car, Farquhar asked if he could come with us when we dropped off the things at the cave. He wanted to talk to Coracle. Dad agreed.

Dad drove the car up to the back building where Farqhhar was staying and where the Anti-G was parked. We transferred the materials into the other car and were off to the cave. When we got there, Farquhar helped us carry all the heavy items up to the top of the hill. We placed the boxes directly over the main chamber, the area we would blow up tomorrow. He was a big help. Even though his muscles hadn't been exercised much since he was resurrected, he was easily able to lift a hundred pounds. After we finished, he asked if he could go talk with Coracle alone.

"Sure," Dad said, handing him a flashlight.

"I will stay inside the cave tonight. I have many questions for Coracle. I shan't go hungry after that enormous late lunch."

"Okay. I'm sure Coracle can help you with anything you might need. See you tomorrow. And by the way," Dad called to his retreating back, "stay in the cave until we come get you. In the morning, you'll need to hide in the smaller chamber where she thinks you are recovering. We'll come back for you later."

He nodded. We watched as he disappeared down the stairs.

When we reached the house, we worried that Effie would ask why we'd come back in a different car, but we needn't have. She and Andrew were busy making dinner in the kitchen.

"Wow!" Dad said. "What a nice thing to do. This looks and smells great."

"We are making a combo dinner, part modern and part Old World," Effie said. "I'm baking the bread and cooking the soup, and

Andrew is roasting the meat."

During the meal, we didn't say much about our trip, except that we found everything. Dad gave Effie her new clothes during the meal. She was so excited that she jumped up and went to try them on. I guess girls are girls no matter what era.

It was probably the best meal we'd had in our new home. Everyone was in a good mood and looking forward to tomorrow.

After dinner, Dad said we should lay out the plans for the next day. It was going to be a big one. We discussed the things we needed to take and the time to leave, but I knew everyone was also wondering what they would say to Coracle before he left. I wasn't quite sure what to say to him. He was going to have to sort out being a machine that had discovered emotions. And now he had the Inventor floating around in his circuits. I think I'll just wish him good luck on his journey and tell him that I hope to meet again in the future.

It had been a relatively easy day, and I spent an hour or so reading in bed. I hadn't done that in a long time. The idea of school was back on my radar screen.

— 22 —

He's on His Way ... and We're on Ours

The alarm clock jolted Dad out of a sound sleep and even woke me in my room. We both got up and made our way to the kitchen. Effie joined us a moment later. We were all eager to get started. Effie asked Dad if the chief was still at the cave.

"Yes," Dad said. I could see his relief that he didn't have to lie. "He is at the cave with Coracle."

"Where is he going to stay after Coracle leaves?" Effie asked.

"He will stay at the cave or ... or maybe we could put him in the building out back. He promised he'd never bother you. If there is any sign of trouble, Farquhar will be moved to another location."

"You don't know this man," Effie said. "He is very determined to get what he wants, in any way possible."

Dad said he knew that. He seemed confident on the outside, but I don't think he had any idea how to handle the living conditions. And how could he? Everything was happening much too fast.

As we were walking out of the house, Andrew came around the corner and said hello, startling us. "Looks like I almost missed you," he said.

"Good to see you, Andrew," Dad said. "Hop in and come along."

Andrew asked me what we were going to do. I took him aside and filled him in on what had happened yesterday with Coracle, Farquhar, and my dad. Andrew couldn't believe that so much had happened in only a day and a half. He was full of more questions as we got into the car and drove to the cave entrance. Didn't this guy ever stop talking? I guess I know how my dad feels about all my questions.

When we arrived, Dad asked Andrew and Effie to bring up the few boxes we hadn't brought yesterday and place them by the other things that were already up there. He and I were going to check on Coracle and be sure the chief was in a decent state to see Effie.

As soon as we reached the top of the stairs, we heard Coracle's usual greeting. The lights came on and we replied, "Good morning to you, Coracle."

We descended the stairs. "Ready to fly?" Dad asked him.

"All systems have been checked and are operational," said Coracle.

Dad was looking around. "Have you seen the chief?"

"Why, yes, we have had many discussions."

"Where is he?"

"Right here with me."

"What?" I said in disbelief. Dad's jaw dropped.

"Farquhar has decided that your world is not where he wants to live, and he asked if I would take him to a place where his skills would be more appreciated. He will be riding along with me. He's inside resting comfortably in suspended animation."

We were stunned, although it did solve the troublesome problem of where to keep him.

"Are there other planets like ours out there?" I asked.

"Yes, there are many planets with primitive life forms, but none as interesting as humans. Farquhar will have to make some adjustments, but he can still be the chief."

I realized that there were many questions about the cosmos that we'd never bothered to ask Coracle, but Dad had always been so preoccupied with the inventions. And I'd been preoccupied with simply adjusting to all these situations. We'd always thought there'd be more time to talk with him. Unfortunately, that time had just run out.

"Will you ever be coming back to Earth?" I asked, realizing that we might be missing a great opportunity to ride along with Coracle to other planets.

"I don't think so. Why?"

"We'd like to go with you and zip around the stars, explore other planets."

"If you wish, I will return at a later date. Perhaps then we can travel together."

"Coracle," Dad said, "I want to thank you for helping my mother have me."

"Glad it worked out, but you should tell that to the Inventor. It was his idea."

"I feel funny saying this to you, but I have really enjoyed talking with you."

"No need to feel that way. It's not your fault that the only intelligent life on this planet is human. There is more out there than anyone can imagine."

Dad looked at his watch, and I knew we had to get back to Andrew and Effie and let them know what had happened to Farquhar. We also needed to start drilling the holes for the explosives. Dad stepped forward, told Coracle goodbye one last time, and wished him well on his next adventure.

We heard a familiar noise. One of Coracle's side panels was opening. Inside the open panel was a thin, square-shaped screen that looked like a tiny computer monitor. "Here is the all the information you ever need for your inventions," Coracle said. "Just ask your question to the screen, and it will prompt you through to the answer." Coracle told Dad that it contained a vast variety of knowledge. "This machine will assist you in many ways; just don't let it fall into the wrong hands."

Dad put the screen into his backpack and thanked Coracle for the resource. It was much more than he had ever anticipated.

"Please send Effie and Andrew down," Coracle said. I could tell that Dad wished he could stay a bit longer, but he had to get to work. I stayed behind to wait for the others.

As Dad was walking away, Coracle said, "Thank you, Neil. I have enjoyed our time together, and if there is ever a real need I will return."

Dad turned around and smiled. "We'll keep that in mind. I'll send the others right down." And with that, he climbed the stairs from the main chamber for the last time.

I was remembering the first time we'd made our way along these passages, how scary and unknown everything was. I wondered if the blast would destroy the tunnels as well as the main chamber, but we would find out soon enough. I couldn't wait to see what it would look like when Coracle blasted through the broken rock and flew away.

I spent my last precious moments alone with Coracle. He gave me lots of good advice, while I, as usual, asked him every question I could about where he'd be going.

After a short wait, Effie and Andrew appeared. Effie told me what my dad had said about the chief leaving with Coracle. She grinned. "Seems this world is just too calm for him." The relief on her face was obvious.

We talked to Coracle for ten more minutes, but I knew we couldn't drag this out much longer. I was afraid it would be impossible to leave if we did. Reluctantly, I hugged Coracle goodbye, which seemed to please him. He'd never experienced that before. His emotions seemed to be growing daily. The others did the same, and with a last farewell, we left the main chamber. I had to hide my moist eyes.

Dad had been measuring and chalking out the exact placement of the holes on the rock, and he told us when we returned that Coracle was exact in his calculations. The drilling went quickly through the sandstone, which was good because we didn't bring any extra gasoline for the generator. Speaking of the generator, he asked how he was going to be able to get it back down the hill without the chief's help.

"Hey, Dad," I said, flexing my muscles. "Isn't that where I come in?"

He grinned as he put the drill back in its box.

"Look what Coracle gave me so I can always remember him," I said, holding out a small, silver-colored coin-like object with an unknown inscription on it. "Coracle drilled a small hole through the top of it and said I should wear it. The charm would come in handy. What do you think he meant?"

He studied it closely. "Your guess is as good as mine."

Effie held out her wrist. "Look what he gave me." It was a beautiful golden bracelet. Different colored stones and metals combined to form an unusual design.

"That's very nice," Dad said. I've never seen anything like it. She was fixated with her wrist, turning it around in the sun. It reminded me of the chief looking at his new knife blade.

"And look at the charm that Coracle gave me," said Andrew. It was similar to Colin's, but the image was different. "He said it would bring me good luck."

"Are you finished with the drilling?" I asked Dad.

"Yes, everyone can put one stick of dynamite into each hole."

We connected all the wires to a box that would set all the charges off at the same time. We lugged the generator and other stuff to the car before positioning ourselves behind a large rock some thirty feet away.

"Colin, do you want to push the button?" Dad asked.

Duh. What eleven-year-old boy doesn't like the thought of blowing up something? "Yeah," I said.

Andrew started the countdown. "Three ... two ... one."

I flipped the switch.

BLAMMMM!

As the dynamite exploded, dust, rock, and debris flew into the air. Then it was eerily silent for a few seconds. A cracking noise suddenly erupted, followed by a large plume of dust rising from the hole and covering us. Fortunately, most of the rubble fell back into the hole.

We were brushing ourselves off when we hear a whirling sound. Coracle rose like a helicopter and hovered about ten feet above the hole. He tipped side to side as if saying goodbye. Then he accelerated at an unbelievable rate and disappeared from sight in seconds.

"I guess that's it," I said sadly. "Back to our normal lives." Then I looked at Effie. "Well, almost normal."

— 23 —

A SINGING SENSATION

We unloaded the drill, generator, and other equipment from the car before heading to the house. We sat down at the kitchen table with glasses of lemonade. I could still taste the dust in my mouth.

Dad looked like he had something to say. "Andrew, it's about time we brought you mother into our inner circle. Will you ask her to join us for dinner tomorrow?"

"Sure, I think she would like to come over." Andrew said.

"It hasn't been right that you've had to keep secrets from her, but things have happened so fast. Let me handle the dinner discussion."

"All right by me."

"Then it's settled. Effie, will you help me with the menu?"

"I would be happy to. It will be nice to have a woman to talk to," Effie said.

The discussion turned to where we thought Coracle had taken Farquhar. I'm sure he had the perfect place in mind. And what about the Inventor? Would he even know that his location had changed, being that he was now electrical energy?

A moment later, Andrew said his goodbyes and left for home.

Effie went to listen to records, and I was reading the welcome packet from my new school. I shouted out pertinent information to

Dad whenever I thought it was important. Dad was trying to figure out the screen that Coracle had given him.

Effie abruptly turned off the music and walked into the kitchen. "Colin and Neil, I've been thinking. I want to be a singer. When I was a girl, I dreamt about singing at the village gatherings but seldom had the chance because Farquhar didn't like me to for some reason. Most of the time, I just practiced as I did my work. I have composed many of my own songs and have memorized all of the old songs used at our tribal ceremonies. I have been listening to the radio, Colin's records, and watching TV. I know that I can be as good as or better than many of those people, but I need your help in planning how to do it.

I have been thinking about how I can fit into my new life. The more I think about it, the more sense this makes to me. I can sing about where I came from to the people I live with now. It's just about the only thing I think I can do in this place, and it happens to be the thing I have always dreamed about doing."

Dad said that neither of us knew very much about the music business, but we would sure find out.

"It would be so much fun to see you on stage," I said.

Effie shrieked with delight. "Thank you! Thank you!" And she left the room singing.

"Colin, do you want to help me manage a pop star?"

"Sure, Dad. I think I would be pretty good at it."

"We'll have to think up a story about her, where she is from, why she is singing these different songs, and what the songs mean," said Dad.

"Let me start, okay? I have some ideas; I'll work with Effie on the plan."

"By all means," he said.

I scooted my chair back and went into the living room. Effie and I talked about how she was going to make her debut into the world of entertainment.

Dad eventually called us back into the kitchen. He had been thinking about some of the things Effie would have to do before going public.

I told him we were already working on that.

He laughed, and then he helped us outline on paper the specific areas Effie needed to work on. English was first on the list.

"I would be glad to work with her," I offered. "It would be nice to not have to worry about these translators."

"And I can teach you the Pic language," she said. She was a hard worker and very determined. I knew she would be speaking English in no time.

Later that evening, my dad walked by the living room on his way to bed and said good night to us. He told Effie that she was now part of our family. "There might be stressful times ahead for you, but we will work them out together."

Effie told us that she was very lucky to have found such good people, that we made her feel at home, and she would never forget what we had done for her. I could see that she was becoming emotional.

When I thought she might start crying, I said good night to her and went to bed, too.

As I lay in bed, I couldn't decide what to think about: school, soccer practice, Effie, my dad and his inventions, the new computer screen, Coracle … My head was spinning when I finally drifted off.

The next morning I awoke to scratching on my window. It was Andrew. I looked at the time. It was eight-thirty. I motioned for him to go around the back to the kitchen. I got up, slipped on some clothes, and walked through the kitchen to unlock the door.

Andrew walked in and said, "I thought I should get here early so I don't miss out on all the action. It seems like if I miss a day, it takes forever just to fill me in."

"I'm planning on a quiet day actually. Farquhar and Coracle are far from here by now," I said. "Oh, I got the new student package, along with the soccer information. I was looking at it last night, but I have lots of questions for you."

"Fire away," Andrew said. We went through the school registration materials, and Andrew told me about the other boys that were in soccer and what they were like. I told him I was more nervous about playing soccer and going to a new school than confronting a crazy sword-wielding warrior.

Andrew hadn't heard any of the last few things I'd said. He was looking at something on the counter. "Hey, it's your dad's new computer screen gadget. Have you tried it? Do you know how to use it?"

"I watched my dad using it, but I don't think he has it figured out yet."

"Come on," Andrew urged. "Let's ask it some questions." I brought the screen back to the kitchen table and pulled my chair closer to Andrew's.

"What should we ask it?"

"I don't know. Let me think." He drummed his fingers on the table. "I know! Let's find out if there is another place like the cave around here. Maybe there are more friendly aliens."

"Be careful what you ask for; you just might get it," Dad said, startling us. He had walked up behind us without either of us hearing him.

"How long have you been up?" I asked.

"Well, good morning to both of you too."

"Sorry, Dad. I didn't mean it that way," I said.

"Oh, I know. I'm just kidding you. You know, Andrew, that's not a bad question. Go on, Andrew, ask away."

Andrew asked the screen if there were any more places on or near this island like the cave that Coracle was in.

"Give it a few seconds," Dad said.

A blinking square appeared, followed by a number of sentences. The answer was yes! There was a general description of the island's shape and size, along with an approximate distance from Coracle's cave. It didn't provide the name of the island, or give the longitude or latitude.

I looked at Andrew and then my dad. "It looks like there are still unexpected things to discover. Do we want to start looking for something that might be even stranger than what we just experienced?"

There was a pause.

"Yes, absolutely," Andrew said.

"What about you, Colin?" Dad asked.

"As crazy as it sounds, my answer is also yes. How about you, Dad?"

"Why not? If we made it through this last ordeal, we can make it through anything."

Then Andrew asked the screen a second question. "Are the aliens in the other hidden place friendly or unfriendly?"

The square blinked again: Not enough information to determine the answer.

"We will just have to keep our eye open and be careful," I said.

Andrew said that he was excited and wanted to begin the search right away. He would have his mother bring over his maps. His huge collection of old maps showed all the area islands, large and small. It would help us narrow down the possible sites using the limited information we had received.

But our attention spans had narrowed. After I finished my chores, Andrew and I were off to the beach to look for objects that had washed up. We had to be back by four o'clock to help with dinner. Andrew's mom would be over around five. I hoped my dad had found a way to tell Amelia about what had been going on.

— 24 —

My New Family

Andrew and I were setting the table, and Dad was moving between the stove and the counter area. He was stirring pots on the stove and preparing a salad.

"Where is Effie?" I asked. "I thought she was going to help with the dinner."

Dad turned from the stove. "She did the prep work. She's in the back building now. If Amelia gets upset by what we tell her, there's no need to include Effie."

"So you think my mom might get angry?" Andrew asked.

"I don't know. We will just have to wait and find out."

The doorbell rang. Andrew and I looked at each other. I guess we wouldn't have to wait much longer.

Amelia jumped right in, grabbing an apron to help. "What do you call this stew?" she asked. "I'm not familiar with this recipe."

"It's a very old recipe. It came out of one of the Inventor's old cook books."

Amelia shot Dad a funny look.

Everything was coming together. A few minutes later, we were sitting at the table, passing dishes and chatting.

Everyone finally finished eating, and it was about time for

dessert. I had a hard time even thinking about cake and ice cream, always my favorite, because I knew time was running out. I was also feeling bad that Effie couldn't eat with us. When was Dad going to start the discussion? Andrew and I stared at the table, and I wondered if we should start setting out the dessert plates.

Dad cleared his throat. "Amelia?"

She looked up and stopped talking.

"Yes, Neil?"

Dad was drawing on the table with his finger. He looked up. "I just can't tell you how great it is to have you and Andrew as neighbors."

She smiled.

"As you know, we haven't been here long and haven't really had time to settle in. There is something I've wanted to tell you, but because everything happened so fast, I didn't know how."

Amelia sat back in her chair expectantly.

"Immediately upon our arrival, unusual things started happening. We received a series of oblique notes from the Inventor. There were references to an event that I was involved in as a kid–right on this property. To tell you the truth, I just thought he was a little crazy. It started with an old book written in some ancient language. It had a map in it."

She nodded. Andrew had told her that much.

"When I saw it as a kid, the map took up two pages. My friends and I copied it and tried to find a treasure, but we had no luck. Well, when I looked at the map recently, I saw that someone had attached an extra page. Colin and Andrew decided to take a shot at finding the treasure, and they found almost all the markers leading to what I thought would be a lost treasure. Now the next events are going to be hard to believe, but let me assure you they're all true."

Amelia nodded her head as if she understood.

"We didn't exactly find treasure, like gold and jewels. What we found was a very intelligent spaceship that had been trapped underground for hundreds of years. Coracle, that's the name of the ship, was the real brains behind the Inventor. I'm sure this sounds crazy to you, but there's more. We found four people that had been put into hibernation by Coracle. There's a long story behind that. We can discuss it later. Anyway, although there were a few scary times, we brought them back to life." He paused, as if to read her expression.

She didn't look disbelieving at all. She just wore an amused look as she waited patiently for him to continue.

"Unfortunately, a couple of those people died. Anyway, we helped Coracle escape his underground prison, and he is traveling somewhere in space. I told Andrew not to tell anyone about this until I could figure things out. That was wrong, I see now. You should have been included, just as Andrew instinctively was." Dad stopped talking and waited for Amelia to say something.

She had a strange look on her face. "Andrew, is what he said really true?"

"Yes, it's exactly how he said."

"This is some kind of joke, right? Well, it's very funny … and clever." She looked around, but no one was laughing. She suddenly seemed to realize that we were serious.

"Andrew, are you sure you're all right?"

"Yes, Mom. The last weeks have been very exciting."

Amelia sat there speechless.

"One more thing." Dad broke the silence. "Of the four people that we brought back, only one remains … and she is living here. You know how you were telling me it would be nice to have a woman friend close by? Well, we have one for you." Dad was smiling.

"Where is she?" Amelia asked.

"Colin, will you go get Effie?"

"Sure, Dad."

"I'll come, too," said Andrew.

"No, you won't," Amelia said protectively. "Stay right here with me."

While I was putting on my shoes, Amelia was doing most of the talking. She said she was upset that Neil had not told her what was going on, but on the other hand, she may have thought he was totally crazy and called the authorities if he had. She said she would need some time to think about this.

As Effie and I were walking up to the back door, I finished telling her what had happened, and that I wasn't sure if Amelia was angry or not.

Effie said she would talk with Amelia and make her understand. She had a strangely powerful look in her eyes. I was glad she was on our side.

I walked in to the kitchen with Effie behind me. I handed a translating device to Amelia. "You will need this to understand her. That is, unless you are fluent in Pic?"

Amelia slipped the earpiece on without question.

"Amelia," Dad said, "I would like to introduce you to Effie. Effie, this is Amelia, Andrew's mother."

"It's nice to finally meet you," Effie said with a warm smile. You have a strong, intelligent boy."

I could see that Amelia was starting to feel more comfortable with the situation. She's the kind of mom that can roll with the punches. I think she was mostly concerned that something bad could have happened to Andrew, and she wouldn't have known anything about it. Amelia visibly composed herself. "Effie, do you like cake and ice cream?"

"Ice cream is my favorite food," Effie said with a huge smile.

"Then have some dessert," Amelia said. "Boys, get help me set the table." As we were serving dessert, Amelia leaned forward and softly told Dad that she should be very angry with him, but for some reason she wasn't. She told him that from that moment on, she would like to be included in any new adventures. She leaned back in her chair, smiled, and was as pleasant as could be.

We enjoyed each other's company as we ate dessert. Everyone was talking and laughing like one big happy family. Not exactly typical, but a family nonetheless.

After everyone was finished, we all drifted to different parts of the house. Dad was finishing with the kitchen clean up, Amelia and Effie were on the couch talking, and Andrew and I were in my room looking at his maps.

Since the screen hadn't given us much in the way of directions, we used the map legend to measure the distance on a piece of string. We then drew a circle around Coracle's cave, making it the center point. The outside of the circle intersected with only a couple of other islands, so it wasn't hard to narrow down which islands we they would need to explore to uncover another mystery. We talked about what we should be looking for and what new questions we should ask the screen.

I looked up from the map to find Amelia and Dad standing in my doorway. "Get your stuff together, Andrew," Amelia said. "It's time to go now."

Dad stepped into the room, looking at the map and then at us. "What are you boys doing with that map and string? Ah, I know. Amelia, you wanted to be included in the last adventure. Well, how about the next one?" She smiled.

As Andrew got his things together, he was telling his mom all about the screen and the questions he had asked it. "Then the answer came right up on the screen!"

She seemed excited by the prospect of exploring a new place, but there was much to do, such as starting school, before we could begin our search.

We said good night to Amelia and Andrew. Dad and Effie were talking in the living room. I went to my room, jumped on my bed, and took out the letter from my new school.

I had a lot to look forward to, including a new school and new friends, soccer, helping Effie with her singing career … and investigating another hidden place that may have contained by extraterrestrials.

* * *

"Hey, Colin?"
I stand and look around my room. No one there. Am I going mad?
"It's me, the reader."

"Okay, reader, what do you want from me?" I ask with outstretched arms.

"I want to know what you are going to find on that other island."

I laugh. "You are just going to have to read the next book to find out."

"Thought you would say that. Why is the reader always the last to know?"

to be continued....

Lightning Source UK Ltd.
Milton Keynes UK
02 November 2009

145720UK00001B/136/A